ABOUT THE AUTHOR

George G. Gilman was born in 1936 in what was then a small village east of London. He attended local schools until the age of fifteen. Upon leaving school he abandoned all earlier ambitions and decided to become a professional writer, with strong leanings towards the mystery novel. He wrote short stories and books during evenings, lunch hours, at weekends, and on the time of various employers while he worked for an international newsagency, a film company, a weekly book-trade magazine and the Royal Air Force.

His first short (love) story was published when he was sixteen and the first (mystery) novel ten years later. He has been a full-time writer since 1970, writing mostly Westerns which have been translated into a dozen languages and have sold in excess of 16 million copies. He is married and lives on the Dorset coast, which is as far west as he intends to move right now.

*The STEELE series by George G. Gilman
and published by New English Library:*

ADAM STEELE 1: THE VIOLENT PEACE
ADAM STEELE 2: BOUNTY HUNTER
ADAM STEELE 3: HELL'S JUNCTION
ADAM STEELE 4: VALLEY OF BLOOD
ADAM STEELE 5: GUN RUN
ADAM STEELE 6: THE KILLING ART
ADAM STEELE 7: CROSS-FIRE
ADAM STEELE 8: COMMANCHE CARNAGE
ADAM STEELE 9: BADGE IN THE DUST
ADAM STEELE 10: THE LOSERS
ADAM STEELE 11: LYNCH TOWN
ADAM STEELE 12: DEATH TRAIL
ADAM STEELE 13: BLOODY BORDER
ADAM STEELE 14: DELTA DUEL
ADAM STEELE 15: RIVER OF DEATH
ADAM STEELE 16: NIGHTMARE AT NOON
ADAM STEELE 17: SATAN'S DAUGHTERS
ADAM STEELE 18: THE HARD WAY
ADAM STEELE 19: THE TARNISHED STAR
ADAM STEELE 20: WANTED FOR MURDER
ADAM STEELE 21: WAGONS EAST
ADAM STEELE 22: THE BIG GAME
ADAM STEELE 23: FORT DESPAIR
ADAM STEELE 24: MANHUNT
ADAM STEELE 25: STEELE'S WAR: THE WOMAN
ADAM STEELE 26: STEELE'S WAR: THE PREACHER
ADAM STEELE 27: STEELE'S WAR: THE STOREKEEPER
ADAM STEELE 28: STEELE'S WAR: THE STRANGER
ADAM STEELE 29: THE BIG PRIZE
ADAM STEELE 30: THE KILLER MOUNTAINS
ADAM STEELE 31: THE CHEATERS
ADAM STEELE 32: THE WRONG MAN
ADAM STEELE 33: THE VALLEY OF THE SHADOW
ADAM STEELE 34: THE RUNAWAY
ADAM STEELE 35: STRANGER IN A STRANGE TOWN
ADAM STEELE 36: THE HELLRAISERS
ADAM STEELE 37: CANYON OF DEATH
ADAM STEELE 38: HIGH STAKES
ADAM STEELE 39: ROUGH JUSTICE
ADAM STEELE 40: THE SUNSET RIDE
ADAM STEELE 41: THE KILLING STRAIN
ADAM STEELE 42: THE BIG GUNFIGHT
ADAM STEELE 43: THE HUNTED
ADAM STEELE 44: CODE OF THE WEST

THE OUTCASTS

George G. Gilman

NEW ENGLISH LIBRARY
Hodder and Stoughton

A New English Library
Original Publication, 1987

Copyright © 1987 by
George G. Gilman
First New English Library
Paperback Edition, 1987

British Library C.I.P.

Gilman, George G.
    The outcasts.—(Adam Steele; 45)
    Rn. Terry Harknett   I. Title
    II. Series
    823'.914[F]   PR6058.A686/

ISBN 0-450-41734-4

Printed and bound in Great
Britain for Hodder and Stoughton
Paperbacks, a division of Hodder
and Stoughton Ltd., Mill Road,
Dunton Green, Sevenoaks, Kent
TN13 2YA, (Editorial Office: 47
Bedford Square, London, WC1B
3DP) by Cox & Wyman Ltd.,
Reading, Berks.

for
TESSA
new to my business,
and family—welcome.

Arlene Forrester was dead.

Adam Steele did not often indulge in what he considered futile sentimentality. But when he stepped out from church the warm summer morning of her funeral he felt palpable sadness fill his throat. This as he saw the scene at the southern end of Main Street was unchanged from when he and the others had followed the coffin into the white-painted clapboard building fifteen minutes earlier.

The old black woman had been known to every citizen of the town in the timber and all who worked the places scattered along the Providence River Valley. Everyone knew she was dead, and it was printed in the *Post-Despatch* that she was to be buried in the stone wall surrounded cemetery of the Providence church this day.

The Virginian had been a little surprised that so few people attended the service within the gleamingly clean, flower-bedecked church. To watch the Broadwater undertaker and his three helpers carry the plain pine coffin up the aisle, rest it on the trestles in front of the altar. Then listen to the Reverend Joseph Marlow say prayers and deliver the eulogy in an insincere monotone while he distractingly ran a forefinger back and forth along the pencil line of his moustache, his deep-set eyes never raising their gaze from the pages of his prayer book: like he was afraid of dire consequences should he slip up over a single word.

Then *Abide With Me* was sung: this hymn always sung at Providence funerals unless a deathbed wish or a request from the bereaved family called for something different.

Arlene Forrester had not realised she was so seriously ill. Then she sank into deep unconsciousness for a period of thirty-six hours: ended by her death. Her only surviving family comprised a preacher brother, Elroy, in Kansas. He had either not received, or did not bother to reply to the wire sent to inform him of his sister's passing.

So Arlene, who had done cleaning, laundering and cooking chores for so many households in and around Providence would have gotten a straightforward county funeral had not Adam Steele and Lavinia Attwood chipped in for a few extra frills.

In addition to making a contribution to the funeral expenses, the Virginian also had a wreath made up by Amelia Decker, the wife of the town butcher who took care of such things hereabouts. And attended the funeral service in his most sombre-hued city style suit.

The schoolteacher had also brought a wreath, made up by a group of her girl students, to be carried atop the coffin. And, because of her staid line of work and sobersided personality, she had little difficulty in dressing appropriately for the solemn occasion: she came to church in full mourning, even wore a hat with a fine mesh veil.

Discounting the Broadwater men, the only other member of the congregation was Sheriff Len Fallows, as immaculately dressed as his wife always insisted he should be. He wore nothing brighter than a light grey vest.

The lawman was even more reticent than Steele in raising his voice for the singing of the hymn and the preacher was dominant in this while his wife, attired in matching clerical black, provided with Miss Attwood a sweeter toned duet.

Thus, since Joe Marlow officiated, Len Fallows was there to represent the county, Jane Marlow lost no opportunity to play the organ and the Broadwater men were being paid for their presence, the Virginian and the schoolma'am were the only true mourners at the funeral of the old black woman.

Outside in the bright sunlight, the air scented more heavily by timber than flowers on the neatly kept graves, Steele was so concerned at what he saw—or the people he failed to

8

see—he absently started to put his black Stetson back on his head: would have done so had Lavinia Attwood not nudged his arm, raised the veil off her angular, lightly-powdered face to show the frown of censure she wore.

Len Fallows, walking immediately behind the undertaker and his men carrying the coffin on their shoulders, did not have the advantage of such a warning, and he donned his hat. Then he looked sharply around, like he sensed he had committed some kind of impropriety, and saw that he had. He spread a scowl across his rough-strewn, black-moustached face, snatched the Stetson off, carried it one handed at his side in the same way as Steele.

Lavinia Attwood cleared her throat with a sound that suggested distaste for the sheriff's lack of reverence, and at the same time satisfaction that he had got back in line.

Steele glanced around, too. But with a purpose: looked for a sign that latecomers were about to gather at the cemetery, the people collecting to at least witness the lowering of the coffin into the ground.

He peered first along Main Street, saw it was deserted except for Jane Marlow who had left the church at the rear of the funeral party, then angled away to go down the gravel pathway, out of the gate and toward the house next door. Where smoke rose out the chimney, obviously from a stove upon which she had set the makings of the Marlows' midday meal.

At a window of the house directly across from the Marlow home, and at the cracked open door of the one next to it, Vera Daltry and the less aged Janet Roper showed their faces. And Steele found himself drawn to the cynical conclusion that these worthy ladies were neither morbidly nor sorrowfully interested in the funeral of Arlene Forrester. Instead watched anxiously to see that nothing was done to mess up the cemetery and the church for which they and a few other christian women held themselves responsible.

Then the rattle of a slow-moving wagon drew Steele's attention out along the red dirt road to the south of town. There were a few farmsteads out there to both sides of the

9

trail, but he saw at once that it was a strange wagon approaching Providence. Hauled by a pair of burros. And the driver of the rig was a Mexican.

A passing-through stranger. Maybe an itinerant hand looking for work hereabouts. It didn't matter to the scowling Steele as he and the others reached the fresh-dug grave, waited for the next stage of the burial ritual. In the far south west corner of the cemetery, still on consecrated ground but as far away from the church as it was possible to get without being outside the stone wall that bounded the lush green area neatly aligned with cross and headstone marked mounds of graves.

The Virginian had known Arlene Forrester well enough to be sure that she had no connections with Mexico or Mexicans: so the man driving the wagon was certainly not heading up the trail as a latecomer to the funeral of the old black woman.

It was the worst part of the interment now, nervous tension acting to stretch time while the undertaker and his men sweated and grimaced and groaned as they lowered the heavy coffin from their shoulders to the side of the grave across from the mound of displaced earth. Under the scrutiny of intently gazing eyes that seemed hypnotically to search for a mistake, a slip that would tilt the box: send it crashing without dignified ceremony too early into the hole.

The wagon came to a halt immediately on the other side of the cemetery wall. And the silence seemed to heighten the concern of the undertaking men, who could do no more than glance irritably toward the distraction before they concentrated again on their chore.

Marlow, Fallows, Miss Attwood and Steele all in some way welcomed the intrusion that drew their attention away from the matter in hand.

Then the tall, thin, very erect schoolteacher once more uttered a sound in her throat. That this time served to adequately convey her feelings without being allied to whatever facial expression existed in back of her veil. She approved of how the Mexican had not only halted his wagon out of respect for the burial, but had also removed his straw sombrero, then

10

directed a warning frown at the two passengers who rode with the meagre freight in the rear of the delapidated rig. These were two small girls of perhaps six and seven, alike enough to be sisters, with a pronounced resemblance to the driver of the wagon that showed they were surely his daughters.

Then Miss Attwood cleared her throat in a manner that drew all attention to her. When she nodded to signal to Marlow, who looked chastened as he hurried to locate a place in his prayer book, found it, began to intone:

'Man that is born of woman has but a short time to live and is full of misery. He comes up and is cut down like a flower. He flees as it were a shadow and never continues in one stay. In the midst of life we are in ...'

While the coffin was lowered slowly into the grave with two lengths of rope, Steele found his thoughts drifting away into the past. First found his mind filled with memories of scenes similar to this and heard voices stridently repeating the familiar words or hesitantly mouthing variations: less solemn but often more appropriate.

Maybe he had not attended so many actual burials: but there had certainly been a lot of death in his past. Started in violent earnest during the War Between the States. Then dogging him along so many trails all the way to this town in the timber. Which he reached, like the Mexican, aboard a wagon. He had just one passenger: a tiny black baby who was directly responsible for him being a mourner at the funeral of Arlene Forrester today.

And, damnit, on that day preparations were being made to bury somebody in this churchyard!

Now in this cemetery there already were buried a number of people who had been his fellow citizens after he settled on the Trail's End spread north of Providence. Along with several people who were unwelcome intruders on the peace and quiet of this California town in a timbered valley of the western foothills of the Sierra Nevadas.

More of them had gone violently than had, like Arlene Forrester, taken sick and died. How many did he have a hand in killing ...?

'Forasmuch as it has pleased Almighty God of his great

mercy to take unto himself the soul of our dear sister here departed, we herefore commit her body to the ground; earth to earth, ashes to ashes, dust to dust, in the sure and certain . . .'

One of the undertaker's men pressed a little dirt into Steele's free hand and the Virginian came abruptly back to the present: took his turn to toss the earth on to the wreath-adorned lid of the coffin in the depth of the hole. Briefly felt he wanted to shake the hand of the man who interrupted his thoughts before he could start to think guiltily about the dying of Chrissy Murchison, Dan Louder, Susannah Lineker, Fred Kenway; who might not be dead and buried in this cemetery, along with the bunch of evil intentioned men who also rested here, had he not ridden up the south trail with a black baby and a wagonload of household chattels looking for a place to put down roots. Almost two and a half years ago.

'Let us pray,' Marlow said. And snapped close his prayer book: able to recite the Lord's Prayer from memory, as were all the others.

This time the preacher's dominant voice was counter-pointed by the softly spoken words of the Mexican children who intoned a prayer in their own language, unobtrusively coached by their father. They ended before the Americans were through and then, as the Mexicans crossed themselves and a clock in a nearby house began to chime the noon hour, Marlow said hurriedly, plainly eager for the formalities to be completed:

'Mr Chambers, on behalf of the county I thank you for your assistance in this sad affair. I'm afraid there is not the usual funeral repast, but you and your men would be welcome to come join my wife and I in——'

'Thanks, Reverend,' the pot-bellied, pale-faced, bug-eyed, quick-to-smile Broadwater undertaker broke in quickly, 'but my men'll be happy to have their refreshment at Mr Krim's place, I'm sure.'

Marlow almost succeeded in hiding his relief that he and his wife were not required to entertain the four men and could

12

eat lunch alone. While Chambers' assistants, relishing the prospect of a stopover at the Golden Gate Saloon rather than a staid meal with the Marlows, hurriedly shed their mourning coats, took up shovels and began to work with a will at refilling the grave.

After checking with a glance at Miss Attwood that it was now all right, Fallows joined Steele in putting on his hat before he said to Chambers: 'I guess the Golden Gate is as good a place as any to complete our business, Chuck? I'll see you there.'

Marlow cleared his throat, expressed more formal gratitude: 'On behalf of the lamentably absent family of the deceased, I also thank you, Miss Attwood, Mr Steele. For taking the time to attend the ceremony, show respect for our departed sister, God rest her soul.'

Then he swung away to leave. But paused at sight of the Mexican and the two small girls who looked far too young to be so solemn faced as they surveyed the scene across the wall with big, dark, round, unblinking eyes.

Marlow added; 'You, too, sir.'

'*Como dice usted?*' the Mexican responded. Shook his head as he replaced his sombrero, muttered something under his breath with an expression on his youthful face that suggested the words were a taunt against himself. 'I beg your pardon, *padre*,' he hurried to translate. 'I and my two daughters—they are Maria and Conchita—we did not know the person who died. We only——'

'I'm grateful you spared the time to wait until we were through,' Marlow broke in, and it was the first genuine-sounding remark he had made since the start of the funeral. 'There are not many who would show such a mark of respect to a stranger.'

Fallows had started to express a scowl of impatience during the exchange. He growled: 'Now you done it, you got no reason to stop in Providence any longer?'

'*Que?*' The Mexican was disconcerted at the unexpected display of animosity by the big-framed lawman who now unfastened his suit jacket, pointedly revealed the badge of his

13

office pinned to the vest underneath. Then he grunted, took up the reins of the burros, nodded vigorously as he acknowledged: '*Si, Señor Sheriff.*'

He endeavoured to conceal anger behind civility while his daughters with youthful frankness showed what they felt: glowered their deep dislike for Fallows.

'What do you think you kids are looking at?' Fallows snapped at them.

The man on the wagon, his true emotions rising close to the surface, glared for a stretched second at Fallows. Then he shifted his gaze to the children, said something in a rasping whisper that caused them to become solemn faced again. But the older sister delayed her father from commanding the burros to start: asked a curt question. Her father looked like he intended to ignore her, then gave a nod of decision, raked his dark-eyed gaze over the face of everyone at the graveside, said:

'I am looking for a woman.'

'You won't find one around here,' Len Fallows snapped.

The youngest, skinniest, ugliest gravedigger sniggered, then blurted: 'You'd best go on to Broadwater, mister. You go to the Blue Moon Saloon in Front Street and you'll——'

'Quit that kinda talk here and now!' Chuck Chambers snarled, directed an apologetic look at Marlow.

If the slightly built, raggedly dressed, thirty year-old Mexican with a strangely immaturely good looking face understood the reference to women of ill repute who worked at a Broadwater saloon he concealed it behind a bland expression as he insisted; 'Has a woman—a Mexican woman—been to this town since——'

'No!' Fallows interrupted. 'I know if any strangers come and go through this town, mister. You're the first Mexican, man or woman, to come by Providence in years.'

The man on the wagon pointedly avoided looking at Fallows. Concentrated his inquisitive gaze upon Marlow, as the preacher transferred his scowl of disapproval from the undertaker's man who spoke of the Broadwater whorehouse to the lawman, confirmed:

14

'The sheriff is correct, *señor*. Although why he should be so uncivil toward you I fail totally to understand.'

'*Muchos gracias, padre*,' the Mexican said, and touched the brim of his sombrero. '*Adios*.'

He set the wagon rolling now, his expression impassive while his two daughters directed deep resentment toward the entire group in the cemetery. Then they peered at the houses they rode past in the same manner, like they considered everyone in Providence to be as despicable as Fallows.

'Yes, just why were you so unspeakably rude to that unfortunate man?' Lavinia Attwood demanded. This as everyone except for the three men filling the grave moved as a group toward the gateway in the front wall of the cemetery.

Marlow pressed: 'I certainly found your attitude most surprising, Sheriff.'

Fallows did not look at either of them when he answered sourly: 'He's Mexican. And I've yet to come across a Mexican I'd trust further than I could see in a burlap sack on a moonless night. Afternoon to you, folks. All right, Chuck. Let's get up to Harry's place, conclude our business.'

He and the wan-faced, rotund undertaker went out through the gateway, to cross Main Street where it became the south trail. Headed for the hearse and a clutch of saddle horses in the grassy meadow next to Vera Daltry's house.

Marlow sighed, shook his head, murmured ruefully: 'I suppose it's inevitable we should have our share of bigots in a town large as Providence. But I'd never have considered Len Fallows to be one of them.'

'Joseph, dear, the meal's about to go on the table!' his wife called and the preacher bobbed his head to Steele, bowed from the waist to the schoolma'am. Hurried toward his house, muttering grimly that people never ceased to surprise him.

Lavinia Attwood said ruefully to Steele who had remained apparently indifferent throughout the exchanges with the Mexican: 'We all know nothing about people ever surprises you, eh Adam?'

'That's surely right most of the time,' the Virginian replied

15

evenly as they watched Chambers steer the hearse through a tight turn, start north along Main Street. Where Fallows waited, then rode his horse alongside the black-painted rig with the frosted glass side panels. 'Walk you back to the Knight boarding house?'

She shook her head and showed regret as she replied: 'I thank you for the kind thought, Adam. But the other day I promised I'd stop by and see Mrs Daltry. Her late sister was once the schoolteacher in Providence, you know? Blanche is not expecting me for lunch and I've cancelled classes for the afternoon.'

Steele had lately become increasingly aware of something many others had suspected for some time: that the schoolma'am was subtly setting her cap at him. So now he was relieved by her response, but managed to hide this behind a neutral expression as he nodded to the less than beautiful woman before she turned and moved with her customary erect carriage toward the house in which the aged Vera Daltry lived.

He waited until she had been invited inside, the door closed, then crossed the street himself. Unhobbled his gelding and swung up into the saddle. Took from a saddlebag a pair of buckskin gloves which for some reason he had felt it inappropriate to wear at the funeral. Put these on before he slowly wheeled the horse, walked him across the street. Halted alongside the cemetery wall to watch as the trio of Broadwater men, sweating from the exertion and the midday heat, working up their thirsts, hurried to complete the burying of Arlene Forrester.

The eldest of the men allowed his younger companions to complete the work. Rested his shovel against the wall, mopped at his sweat beaded face, donned his mourning coat, said to the mounted man:

'According to Mr Chambers, she was a pretty old lady, mister?'

'Right,' Steele answered absently.

'Death ain't so bad if the person's old, I always think,' the sympathetic man said. 'Not tragic, like when——'

'Yeah, feller,' Steele broke in. 'Even better, Arlene Forrester died in her sleep.'

The undertaker's man showed a fleeting smile as he nodded, agreed: 'That sure is even better, I'd say.'

The Virginian shifted his gaze from the mound of earth that for some time would be an ugly scar on the even green of the surrounding grass. Surveyed the entire cemetery as he drawled: 'It's not usual for people to do that around me.'

'Should I understand what you're sayin', mister?' the oldest man said, a little nervously, as the others picked up their coats but did not put them on. Sloped the shovels to their shoulders.

Steele ran gloved fingertips over the engraved gold plate screwed to the side of the stock of the Colt Hartford rifle that jutted out of the boot hung forward on his saddle. Answered; 'Talking about dying.'

'Yeah, I know, mister, but——'

Steele nodded, said: 'Naturally.'

2

Steele purposely avoided taking any of the short cuts to the shack where Arlene Forrester had lived; elected to go by the longest route, stayed on the streets of the town.

Just beyond the lower end of Main, where it became more like a back country trail featured occasionally with houses and intersected by side roads to places deeper in the timber or up on the flanks of the valley, he was overhauled by the Broadwater funeral men. They were riding their mounts at speed, the faster to get to the square on the north side of town where the sparse but nonetheless welcome comforts of the Golden Gate Saloon awaited.

When they were gone, with no more than uneasy glances toward Steele, and the thud of cantering hooves faded from earshot, just the less obtrusive sounds of the gelding's slow progress and an infrequent snatch of birdsong disturbed the tranquil stillness of the afternoon. And this near silence seemed to emphasise in Steele's mind the total lack of interest shown in him as he rode at a measured pace up the meandering street to where Mission Farm Road cut off to the west. Likewise along this narrower, straighter thoroughfare to where a wagon-wide track cut back southward again, through dense timber: going no place else except the clearing on the back of the gently running Providence River where Arlene's dilapidated one-room shack stood.

Perhaps the deserted look of the town in the timber was nothing more than he should expect, he reflected sourly after he had turned on to the track that led to Arlene's place. After the ill-attended funeral showed nobody gave any kind of a

18

damn that the old Negress was dead. Or, anyway, whether out of lack of interest or the need to pay heed to the midday meal, why should the people of Providence not ignore him?

It was satisfying to think, though, as he reached the clearing beside the sun-glinting river, that maybe some of the good people of this town felt the need to hide their shame as they saw him ride by. Such a theory gave him a childish kind of triumph, but definitely a gratifying brand.

Only when he dismounted out front of the crudely built log shack did he consciously consider the reason he was here. At a place he came to so seldom during Arlene's lifetime: the last, and most vividly recalled, when he was in such desperate need of a different kind of help to that which the old black woman usually provided. When he was wanted for murder.

But that was long in the past.

He moved inside the shack that was spartanly furnished with the basic necessities of hard life for an old black woman, past sixty years, who spent more time at the homes of other people than in her own. Neat and clean, with a place for everything and everything in its place. The only dirt, that which had accumulated since she took sick with a fever while she was cleaning the town meeting hall and came home early to rest up.

To be found the next day by one of Lavinia Attwood's students, sent here because Arlene had not shown up as expected to help with the morning chores at the Knight boarding house, where the schoolteacher roomed.

Thadius Mackay, neither the best nor the worst doctor in California, had given Arlene some medicine. This had cooled her fever but also sank her into a day and a half of hovering between restless sleep, and comatose unconsciousness. From which, Mackay warned, she had no better than a fifty-fifty chance of recovery. She lost.

So did the town, in Steele's view. But, he admitted as he looked down at the open Bible which was one of Arlene's few luxuries—though she probably had regarded it as an essential—nothing was lost that would make too much difference to too many people. Once they had made their new arrangements to do for themselves or have done by some-body else those onorous tasks the black woman had always undertaken so industriously and, invariably, cheer-fully.

Steele felt himself drawn back outside again and for awhile he hunkered down on the bank of the slow-moving river, his back to the shack, his mind empty of thoughts about Arlene Forrester. Except in terms of the gap her death had left in his life.

He would now have to do all his own cooking, cleaning and laundering. Chores, he had to allow, he had managed to take care of before he came to Trail's End and set up home there. But since then he had certainly gotten used to having someone like Arlene around the place, even if only for a few mornings a week.

If he felt he needed to replace her, how was he to do so? Advertise in Huey Attrill's newspaper, maybe? But there was a danger that this would attract some husband-seeking females. And if a likely looking prospect showed up—as willingly available as Lavinia Attwood but a whole lot younger and prettier—would that be a bad thing?

He rose suddenly, scooped a chunk of rock off the ground. Hurled it forcefully out across the river, timed the venting of a curse to coincide with the splash of the stone in the water.

He'd get by, damnit! Maybe his meals would not to be so varied or wholesome, there'd be a little more dust in the house than usual and he would not be so crisply turned out when business brought him to town. But he'd sure get by. And as for taking a wife ...?

Hell, on the day of a funeral it was not the time—and here at Arlene's old shack was surely not the place—to consider such a thing.

Too, it struck him with a stab of shame as he went back into the cabin, he should not think of Lavinia Attwood in the unflattering way that he had. She was much more than just a straight up and down, far from young, prim and proper spinster who saw him as a marriage prospect: had only attended the funeral, maybe, because she knew he would be

20

there. Much more: and it was brutally cruel to think of her in such a way.

While, from a totally selfish viewpoint, it was stupid to contemplate getting on the wrong side of Lavinia. For she was now the one individual in the entire Providence River Valley he could trust without reservation. It was she who, at the very start, had proved to be a true friend in the worst of bad times. And there had been just two others like her: poor retarded Billy Baxter who had died so violently and uselessly, and Arlene.

The rest of the people in the valley fell into two categories as far as he was concerned: represented by Joseph Marlow and Len Fallows. Those like the preacher had accepted the Virginian's presence as a *fait accompli*. Maybe many of these still didn't like the idea of a man they considered a not entirely reformed gunslinger living amongst them. But, not least based upon the way in which Steele had helped to handle valley troubles since he came to Trail's End, they were invariably willing to be civil toward him, even display the warmth of a kind of friendship when the situation required it.

The rest—and at least it was the lesser number—shared the opinion of the lawman. Though, like the others they might acknowledge that Steele had proved invaluable in dealing with violent trouble, they would always resent him for what they were sure he had been, and were certain he always would be. They held the view that men of the kind Steele had been—and still was—attracted trouble like a magnet attracted iron filings: and had he not settled at Trail's End, the trouble which came here after he did would have stayed away.

Such people were barely civil to him, avoided having to talk with him whenever possible and considered that, useful as he had been in troubled times, active help was no more than he should be expected to give.

This afternoon such notions came unbidden to Steele and most went the same way; sometimes needed to be consciously ousted from his mind as he moved about the tiny shack and carefully collected together anything that seemed to be of a personal nature that belonged to Arlene.

It did not amount to much. Enough to half-fill one of the burlap sacks which Arlene had used for picking up dirty laundry. Just the Bible from the crate beside the head of the bed, unmade from when she had died in it, some articles of her Sunday best clothing, a few ornaments and artefacts that were trash to Steele and probably to anyone except Arlene to whom they had been treasures. And one set of baby clothes he knew she had made for Zachery Petrie, the baby boy Steele had brought to Providence who turned out to be kin to Arlene: lived with her until she found a new home by way of her preacher brother Elroy in Kansas.

When he went out of the shack, closed the door behind him and swung up astride his gelding, tied the slackly filled bag to the saddlehorn, he felt conscious of a task well done. It did not matter why, but he had sensed a compulsive need to come here and to do this. So that now, if no one ever came to live in the shack and it rotted from neglect over the years, nothing Arlene had treasured would decay with the fabric of the building. Not here in Providence, anyway.

He rode without a backward glance back along the track. No longer concerned with the shack that now contained nothing which could be associated with Arlene: except for memories. And Steele had tried over so many years to dispense with memories. Especially since he put down his roots on the Trail's End spread where the future could be so bright.

Soon, Arlene Forrester would be a part of the forgotten past. For his mind invariably insisted that he think only bad thoughts of the past. And there were no such memories of Arlene, except for the way she died and was buried.

In truth, his past had not been all bad: but it certainly seemed his mind stored with greater vividness those images of the past that were painful to reflect upon.

It was not until he rode off the end of Main Street, on to the square that was downtown Providence, that he realised with a disconcerting jolt just how far the afternoon had progressed toward evening: how much time he had spent in quiet

22

reflection and disturbing thoughts within the shack and out on the river bank.

There was still sunlight on the square, lined around three sides by buildings, the south side enclosed by the timber from which he emerged. But it had shaded from yellow to crimson, the intensity of its heat was gone and the shadows it cast toward the north east were long, grotesquely distorted.

But the places where he needed to do business were still open.

First he went to the Kenway Hardware Store, one of the row of premises fronted by a raised sidewalk on the east side of the square. The establishment was efficiently run by Faith Kenway since her husband died of a heart seizure at the height of some explosive trouble in Providence. The store stocked the necessary materials to make up a sturdy package of Arlene Forrester's belongings and it pleased the owner to wrap, tie and seal the parcel.

The aging Faith Kenway who had a dual reputation in town—as a teller of fortunes and as its ugliest woman—talked all the time while she provided this additional service, without once touching upon the morning funeral. Until Steele took out money to pay for the materials, when she assured:

'There'll be no charge, Mr Steele. I couldn't make it down to the church to see that poor black woman laid to rest, so please allow me to make this small contribution to your act of kindness?'

Steele shook his head, placed a dollar bill on the counter, told her evenly: 'You're like everyone else who knew Arlene Forrester, ma'am. You could have made it, but you didn't want to make it.' He held up the package. 'I'm grateful for this.'

'But I——' the extremely homely woman started to defend anxiously as Steele headed toward the doorway. But when he paused on the threshold, peered back at her through the twilight of evening in the unlit store, she saw something in the set of his dark eyes she read as an accusation: against which she decided she could offer no rebuttal.

'I'm sorry,' she murmured lamely at length.

'That's good,' he countered, went out of the store.

He rode the gelding through the fading light of evening across the broad square, from the centre of the row of stores on the west side to the combined stage line depot and telegraph office that with the Golden Gate Saloon formed the north east corner.

He glanced into Harry Krim's place as he dismounted, hitched the reins to the saloon's rail which was the only one on his side of the square. Saw that business was slow at this time of day. Harlan Grout, who ran the livery and Tom Knight, husband of Blanche who did most of the work at their boarding house, were in there. Along with the town butcher, Roland Decker, who ran the other two a close race for a triple dead heat as town drunks. The three of them, along with the saloon's owner, were suddenly brightly illuminated by the yellow glow of the kerosene lamps that Krim began to light. The Broadwater undertaker and his men were long gone for their home town. Len Fallows, never one of Krim's regular customers, had also left the saloon.

Michael Morrison, who with his mother Joanne operated the depot of the San Francisco and Central California Stageline Company—along with the telegraph that was extended from Broadwater to Providence earlier this year—was just about to close up the premises for the night when Steele arrived on the threshold.

One of those most strongly aligned with Fallows rather than Marlow in his attitude toward Steele, Morrison was this evening grudgingly helpful as he accepted the package, said he knew Elroy's address in Kansas from when he sent the wire about Arlene's death and would see to it the parcel was correctly marked, put aboard the next stage scheduled to turn around at Providence, two Fridays hence.

Unlike Faith Kenway, Morrison—small of stature, ineffectual looking, almost forty years old and a confirmed bachelor—made no attempt at conscience salving by offering to cover the cost of freight himself. Probably because he had no conscience in the matter; which was all right with Steele,

24

who knew the Morrison mother and son were a more or less self-contained family unit in town: had little contact with other people outside of business and so owed no allegience to anyone in Providence.

His self-imposed chores completed, Steele was now suddenly aware of the uncomfortable emptiness of a day in which he had eaten nothing since breakfast out at Trail's End: and that had been only coffee and a couple of scrambled eggs.

Fleetingly, as he emerged from the stageline depot, he considered stepping into the Golden Gate. Where Harry Krim did not usually provide food for his patrons. But he did make passable coffee that would maybe serve to stop Steele's belly rumbling too loudly until he got back to the spread.

Of course, Blanche Knight sometimes was willing to serve her fine food to people who did not board there: but Lavinia Attwood would be eating supper in the dining room of the boarding house.

In the end, he decided to head straight on home. Was up astride the unhitched gelding when the door of the law office opened to catch his attention and he looked to the side as Len Fallows emerged from the darkened building where he had apparently been sitting alone at his desk in the gathering gloom of evening. The sheriff showed no sign that he had seen the Virginian, walked with his head hung down as he came past the newspaper office toward the saloon. Until he drew close, when he looked up to show a scowl, announced:

'I got good reason not to like Mexicans, Steele.'

He turned toward the batwinged entrance of the Golden Gate. Steele said with a shrug:

'Your business isn't my business, feller.'

'Right,' Fallows said emphatically, like he had made a final telling point in a long and heated argument. Then he peered in over the tops of the Golden Gate's batwings to demand: 'Harlan, you put that shoe on my horse?'

'I sure as hell have, Mr Fallows,' the stockily built livery-man and blacksmith, running to fat and younger than he looked, answered eagerly. 'Be right with you.'

'Stay where you like to be best!' Fallows growled sourly,

glared a share of ill humour at the undeserving Grout before he swung away from the saloon threshold, angled across the corner of the square to the livery separated from the stageline depot by Ethan Brady's First Providence Town Bank.

'You'll pay me tomorrow, I guess?' Grout yelled morosely from the saloon, his voice no more slurred than usual, for he managed to pace his drinking throughout the day to maintain a constant state of drunkenness just a step away from being sober, which enabled him always to do his work efficiently.

'That way it'll stay out of Harry Krim's cash drawer a few more hours!' Fallows countered grimly.

The broad-shouldered, pot-bellied, sandy-haired saloon-keeper growled something in response to the taunt, but by then Steele was too far away to hear Krim's voice as anything but a low grumbling sound. Moments later, as the sheriff entered the livery, Steele rounded the corner of the law office and lock-up which with the meeting hall flanked the start of the north trail out of Providence. That went to Broadwater ten miles away and eventually led to San Francisco, almost three hundred miles distant. The Timber Creek spur that gave access to Trail's End was only about half a mile to the north.

It was the fine summer evening of a hot day. A pleasant, comfortable kind of time. During which the Virginian began to experience satisfying peace of mind now he was through with the burying of Arlene Forrester and had done what he considered necessary to tie up the loose ends of her life. He was hungry still, but the feeling was not too demanding: and the very fact that he could head for his own home, cook up a mess of something to fill his empty belly, itself contributed to the sense of well being.

God rest her soul, as Joe Marlow had said: but without Arlene to come to Trail's End any more, he could please himself entirely when, what or whether he ate. And when or whether he cleaned up afterwards tonight or tomorrow, or...

Hell, to think he had contemplated, even for a few moments, taking another wife...?

'*Señor*, I humbly apologise to you.'

26

It was the Mexican stranger at the funeral. Standing beside a tree just off the trail to the left. Speaking anxiously, almost fearfully: a tightly gripped revolver hanging down at his side. He waited, chewing his lower lip, until Steele had reined in the gelding a few feet away, before he went on:

'For the *momento*, I was afraid you were the sheriff. Come to order me and my girls further away from the town and I——'

'There's no harm done, feller,' Steele interrupted the desperate looking man who stood beside his night camp in a small clearing. 'So take it easy, uh?'

'*Muchos gracias, señor!*' He abruptly realised that the ancient looking revolver which he had earlier aimed at the approaching rider—Steele thought it was an old Army or Navy Colt of war vintage—was still in full view. With clumsy haste he hid it behind his back, grinned foolishly at the Virginian. Started to go on: 'It is good to know...'

He now realised how inappropriate was his expression, switched to the extreme of a morose frown as he completed: '——that not every Anglo in this *valle* hates us because we are Mexicans. My name, *señor*, is Esteban Garcia. You will do me the honour to stay awhile with us, *por favor*? Accept my humble hospitality. We have eaten early, because of the children, you understand. The coffee is now cold and stale, but I can light the fire, uh? To——'

'I'm grateful to you, but I'm almost home,' Steele told him evenly as he completed his survey of the Garcia night camp. Saw that the Mexican had done as much as he could within the limit of his resources to make himself, his daughters and his burros comfortable for the night.

The camp was on the west side of the trail, near a point where the Providence to Broadwater road curved close to the Providence River that could be heard gently trickling on its slow course southward.

The elderly and much repaired wagon had had most of its freight off-loaded: this largely comprised a number of circular whetstones with wooden handles, a frame in which they fitted and a chair on which Esteban Garcia sat while he

27

was operating the blade-sharpening machine. Then a sheet of patched burlap had been draped over some posts to form a ridge tent on the rear of the wagon.

The two small girls were already bedded down within the shelter on the wagon, but they were not sleeping, Steele knew. For after a surreptitious double take he was sure that at least one pair of mistrustful eyes peered out through the moonlit darkness at him.

Beyond the wagon a pair of burros lay contentedly on a patch of grass of which they had obviously cropped their fill.

Esteban, Maria and Conchita Garcia had eaten hot food cooked on a fire in a circle of stones that was now reduced to a heap of grey ash, just a spot of glimmering red here and there in the embers. There was still, Steele thought, the final fading traces of the aroma of cooked meat, chilli flavoured, and strong coffee mixed in with the fragrance of the surrounding woodland. Or maybe, he allowed, his hunger conjured this up in his imagination.

Then all other scents in the night were masked by the not unpleasant aroma of tobacco smoke as the Mexican lit a cheroot. This after he had backed away from the tree at the side of the trail, until he was up against the wagon. The revolver was not in evidence now.

There had been no hollow thud of the heavy metal gun against the wooden bed of the wagon, and now, since Steele was no longer preoccupied with his sense of well being to the exclusion of all else, his mind was clear to be conscious of watching eyes: maybe the threat of a gun levelled at him. Minutes before, while Esteban Garcia had him covered from behind the tree, he had been oblivious to such signals of imminent danger. He said, as Garcia shook out the match, tossed it into the near dead embers of the fire:

'Feller, I reckon even your eldest daughter is too young to handle a firearm. Or maybe you've brought her up differently?'

'*Que?*' He was genuinely perplexed, had obviously not been listening too closely to what Steele said while he relished contentment with the cheroot, relief that what seemed a dangerous situation had turned out fine. Now he realised that the slow-talking American astride the docile gelding had spoken in a tone that carried an understated but nonetheless definite threat. Dug deeply into his memory for the words that had been spoken as he stared hard at Steele, saw where the Virginian peered fixedly, swung around.

He ripped the cheroot from between his teeth, replaced his quiet smile with a glower, rasped something that sounded like a curse. Then spat out a string of fast phrases in Mexican Spanish that were heavy with chagrined parental authority.

This triggered a low-toned exchange between the two small girls within the darkness of the burlap cover. And the wagon rocked on its springs, the burlap billowed, like the children were engaged in a tussle. Maybe for possession of the revolver.

Then one of the girls shouted in a tone of angry resentment. But next was ingratiating, and Steele thought he could guess the gist of what was said. Had his assumption confirmed when Garcia cut across the child's pleading excuse with a harsh command, turned to look intently at the Virginian as he explained:

'Forgive us, *por favor*? All of it is my fault. I am embarrassed to have pointed the *pistola* at you. Like the *vieja anciana*... *Entender*? Like the old woman, you understand, who is afraid of shadows in the night. I tried to rid myself of the *pistola* in a way that is *ingenioso*. My daughters , they are still awake. They are very young. Not so trusting of others as children young as they should be. Little has happened to make them trusting, *señor*. This, too, is my fault. Conchita— the eldest by a year—she thinks she is protecting me. Should you be like the others in the town... Perhaps worse. Will do bad things to us and——'

'Sure, I've got the picture, feller,' Steele interrupted. 'But now you know you and your daughters don't need to be afraid of me. Be on my way home. *Buenas noches*, Garcia.'

Steele made to heel his horse forward, but paused when the Mexican took a hurried step toward him, blurted:

'*Con permiso, señor*! I know what you are sure to reply but I must ask something of you! You are one of so few to have no *aversion* for us. All afternoon I work for the people of your town. To *afilar*——' He looked frustrated, performed a simple mime with both hands, then grunted with satisfaction, pointed to the frame with a whetstone resting on it. '*Si*, I sharpen their blades of all kinds. They are *satisfecho* with the work I do for them. But they do not like me because I am a Mexican.'

Steele was mildly surprised so many of his fellow citizens shared Len Fallows' prejudice toward Mexicans. He said absently: 'Like Joe Marlow—the minister at the funeral, feller—and the lady who was there, I can't explain either why that should be.'

Garcia shook his head vigorously, then dismissively waved his hand holding the cheroot that had gone out. 'I have no interest in this, *señor*.' He shrugged his narrow shoulders. 'It happens in many Anglo towns. I have grown used to this. I have taught my daughters not to let such things make them unhappy. No, *señor*. It is that such people, who have no liking for us, perhaps they do not answer my questions truthfully. So I ask you, *señor*: have you seen a Mexican woman in this *valle*?'

'No, feller.'

'She is my wife,' Garcia hurried on, lifted his face toward the night sky, like he was making a silent plea to heaven while he willed a positive response from Steele. 'The mother of Conchita and Maria, you understand? Her name is Carmelita and she is most beautiful. I do not say this just because she is my wife. You have seen our daughters? Seen how handsome they are, which comes from their mother. You know I do not make foolish claims for them just because they are my daughters?'

'Feller, I——' Steele started.

'It was a year ago she left our village in Baja California, *señor*,' Garcia pressed on, shifting his intense gaze from the moonlit, star-spread sky to the face of Steele, his own features contorted by an expression that conveyed he had difficulty

30

holding back the tears of his misery. 'To seek the fortune that I—a simple *afil* . . . a sharpener of blades—could not provide. She came here to American California. She was seen three months ago. At a place many miles south of this town of Providence. There she worked as the *doncella* . . . the servant, at a *hacienda*. On a big ranch. To earn money to travel further north. I am certain my Carmelita came here, *señor*. Perhaps stayed here. To work for more——'

'No, feller.'

But it is only the *sentido comun* that she came this way to——'

'Easy,' Steele cut across the demanding voice.

'But I——'

'Shut up, Garcia!' Steele snapped as the man seemed in danger of slipping into hysteria. And he was again disconcertingly aware of hostility directed at him from within the burlap shelter on the wagon. Maybe, he reflected anxiously, there was even an immature hand on the butt of the big old Colt, too.

Garcia swallowed hard, nodded vigorously, said hoarsely: 'Please, you will forgive me, *señor*? I try so hard. Not to lose hope. Not to become angry. I thought we were so close to finding my Carmelita here. Of course, I believe a fine, honest man such as you, *señor*. You will forgive me for the way I——'

'That's good,' Steele said. 'That you believe me. So listen to me. No Mexican woman, far as I know, has been through this valley in the past two and a half years. That's as long as I've been living here. That doesn't mean for sure there hasn't been a woman named Carmelita Garcia through this way. But if anyone saw her, I reckon I'd have heard about it. Seeing as how so many people around here don't like Mexicans. It would have been a topic of conversation if one showed up in Providence. Strangers are pretty thin on the ground hereabouts.'

'*Si, señor*.' He bobbed his head rapidly.

'Fine.'

'I truly believe you, *señor*.'

31

There was a fast, rasping exchange on the wagon.

'Fine,' Steele said again. And grinned as the final traces of controlled anger drained out of him. Added: 'You sure ought to.'

'*Si, señor*.' Garcia took out a match with a shaking hand.

Steele angled his horse to the side, heeled him forward. The Mexican was abruptly afraid again and took a backward step, his hands frozen in the act of replacing the dead cheroot between his teeth and striking the match to relight it. He gazed hypnotically at Steele as the Virginian leaned down from his saddle, grasped the handle of the whetstone in the frame. Gave it a forceful turn that sent it into a fast, squeaking spin. He broadened his grin, explained to the disconcerted Garcia:

'I don't have an axe to grind.'

3

From the ten-mile distance of Providence Adam Steele haboured a feeling of ambivalence toward Broadwater. And whenever he rode into the bustling town on the shore of the Providence Lake he invariably needed to temper a charge of expectation with the conscious argument that he was doing just fine on the Trail's End spread.

In area the town was smaller than Providence: it stretched for a mile and a half in a quarter mile strip along the shore of the lake's eastern side, at the base of a steep slope that was the first genuine mountain beyond the western foothills of the Sierra Nevadas. But it was far larger in population: a compact community, its houses and business and civic establishments of many kinds closely packed along Front Street that followed the curves of the lakeside, California and Pacific Avenues that ran in parallel straight lines to the east of Front, and the dozen or so side streets that intersected these wider, longer thoroughfares.

Broadwater was founded back in the days of the gold rush when enough paydirt had been found in the surrounding hills to make it a boom town: the widest open for miles around, supplying the needs and catering to the pleasures of claim stakers who were drawn in from countless miles in every direction. And unlike so many other gold fever communities in California and elsewhere, Broadwater suffered little more than a hiccup when the paydirt in the immediate locality ran out.

Nuggets and dust continued to show up in creeks and be uncovered in the ground for a long time after the rich lodes were exhausted and the grubbers who struck it lucky were eager to travel long distances to indulge in the delights of Broadwater. While many of those who hit the jackpot early decided to settle on the rich farming and grazing land in the lakeside area and the hill country beyond: made more money in their new lines of business for which the merchants and entrepreneurs of Broadwater were avariciously eager to provide services and pleasures.

The fine summer morning of the day after Arlene Forrester was buried, as Adam Steele drove a flatbed wagon with two horses in the traces toward Broadwater for the latest of many visits, he knew it would be nothing like the rip-roaring, wide-open town he had been told it once was. But by Providence standards—which had become his standards—Broadwater was the kind of town inclined to make him feel, deep down in his bones, that he would like to have given a whirl to a different lifestyle. And such notions made him feel guilty: thus did he both love and hate the town.

The trail from the south curved around a towering timber-and brush-cloaked wedge of dirt and rock then ran down a gentle slope, the higher expanse of which was covered with trees. Until abruptly the trail emerged from the pines, and travellers had a bird's eye view of the lake to the left two miles wide and three miles long, the mountain on the right and the town between.

Steele knew Broadwater so well because of the several times he had needed to come to the town since he settled at Trail's End: and often during such visits, when things were not so good as they were now, he had been sorely tempted to abandon conscious argument against the impulses which made the place so compellingly attractive to him.

He knew that beyond the town limits marker the trail became California Avenue, lined with houses that got progressively grander toward the north until, at the far end before the town thoroughfare became open trail again, they were virtual mansions. With lots of space between them, the carefully tended grounds featured with plantings that hid each house from its neighbours. And many were screened

34

from the avenue by high walls or fences or thick-growing hedges. But it cost money to live anywhere along California Avenue: a fortune to afford and maintain a house at the north end.

And he sure had no hankering for Pacific Avenue, where the poor—and the very poorest—citizens of the community lived. The clerks and counter hands, barkeeps and tellers, the broom pushers and maids, saloon girls and croupiers, the out-of-luck gold grubbers and busted gamblers. The men and women, and kids, who worked for the wealthy people who lived on California: or the patrons who had overspent in the business establishments operated by the California Avenue rich along Front Street that swept in two long curves beside the sandy shore of Providence Lake.

It was just occasionally that Steele allowed himself to be drawn to Front Street, the expanse of smooth water on one side, the great variety of business and civic premises on the other.

A half dozen saloons. One restaurant that specialised in steak cuts, another in lake-caught fish. Two hotels, three boarding houses. A casino with all kinds of games of chance. Stores that stocked everything anybody needed, much that they did not unless they had plenty of money to squander. The sheriff's office and jailhouse. The stage line depot. Three livery stables. Four banks. Charles Chambers' funeral parlour. The telegraph office. Two churches and a chapel. The office and printing plant of the Broadwater *Herald-Times*. And the Blue Moon Saloon: of which one of the undertaker's men had spoken at Arlene Forrester's funeral yesterday.

This brick-built place which rose three stories, with balconies around three sides of both upper floors dominated the town from its prime situation midway along Front Street. It was, indeed, a saloon. But it also had a gambling casino, a ballroom and a restaurant. And a string of whores who were considered the best in Broadwater: better even, some said, than were available in the finest houses of San Francisco.

But such high class cost high prices. If a man could not

afford the best, though, there were many other places in Broadwater where the pleasures of the flesh were available for less. And not only in the saloons. For if a man were to approach the right informant he would be steered away from the brightly lit, noisy places on Front Street. To any of a number of dingy back or upstairs rooms along the squalid length of Pacific Avenue where women in other lines of regular business, or newly arrived in town, or just fired, were available.

Too, it was rumoured, women were sometimes for sale behind the respectable façades of California Avenue. Never cheap, but usually clean: the wives or daughters of men whose businesses had fallen on hard times. It was said, also, that behind the high hedges and landscaped front yards of certain houses at the north end of California Avenue, there were women who would pay for the company of a man.

But it had never been the professional whores or the loose or desperate women of Broadwater who had tempted Steele to throw in his hand at Trail's End, move to this town which offered so many types of entertainment. This when he lay in bed unable to sleep, or sat reflecting on his life, or dealt with irksome ranch troubles, or elected to ignore the less than subtle hostility directed at him by certain Providence people. The temptation stronger still when he rode up here: to send a telegraph in the days before Providence had the facility, do business at the Stockman's Association House, to pick up or despatch merchandise at the Broadwater Freight Line Company which did not have sufficient call in Providence to run a wagon ten miles down the trail.

He was only human, sure: and he considered himself as red-blooded as the next man. So it was appealing for him to contemplate the nearness of fine-looking, sweet-smelling, easy-smiling, body-swaying, readily-available women.

But it was the games of chance staged in so many Broadwater establishments that were at the root of the dissatisfaction with his lot sometimes when he thought about or came to this town. For he was a natural-born gambler of the kind who derived little pleasure from the penny ante poker games played in the Golden Gate Saloon. Here in Broadwater, in a dozen places along Front Street, a man could gamble as much as his credit was good for in every kind of no-limit game.

Today, though, as he held the two-horse team to a walk down the lower slope of the hill south of Broadwater, his hat brim tilted low over his forehead to keep out some of the noon sun glare reflected off the lake, Steele found it easy to resist the temptations of the pleasure to be had in poker games that would soon be dealt, at the crap tables where dice would shortly start to roll or the roulette wheels that were about to spin now that last night's participants had slept off the effects of their early hours excesses. For he had come to Broadwater for a kind of business purpose that was a lot more pleasurable than usual.

The house on the Trail's End spread was just a one room place, not much larger, though more substantially built, than Arlene Forrester's shack. It had served the purposes of the Sanderson couple before they took off for no reason that Steele had been able to discover. And it had suited the Virginian for the past two and a half years: probably would have been adequate for the rest of his life. But after he had built up his breeding stock of stallions and mares, sold some foals for good prices and reduced the loan he owed to Ethan Brady to a negligible amount, he was starting to see a profit. And since he had no ambition to amass a cash fortune, he had decided the hard work over long hours merited reward in the material terms of a little luxury.

So he had started to extend the house: added on a bedroom at the rear. And when this was finished he intended to partition the existing room into a separate kitchen and parlour. These changes would require additional furniture, which was why he was driving the wagon into Broadwater this fine summer morning.

For he had read a notice in the Providence *Post-Despatch* announcing a sale of household effects in Broadwater, following the death of one Porter S. Calendar. And from questions put to Tom Knight, Thadius Mackay and two

Providence farmers who had personal or business connections with Broadwater, he had learned Calendar had been a druggist in the town. A sober, cautious, studious bachelor of forty-five or so who, Steele reckoned, might very well have furnished his California Avenue house in just the style he favoured for himself at Trail's End.

Although several competing clock chimes rang out the noon hour as Steele drove the rattling flatbed past the town limits marker and on to California Avenue, there was still a quality of lethargy clamped over Broadwater, which never came fully awake until the sun went down. But there should have been some kind of activity, he thought, a few houses up the street from where he saw the number fifty-seven on a house to the left. For the sale of the late Porter S. Calendar's furniture was scheduled, according to the advertisement in the Providence newspaper, to take place at twelve thirty at number sixty-five California Avenue. But there was as yet no gathering of people, no horses or wagons in the vicinity of the property.

Then he saw that his first thought—that the wrong address, date or time had been printed by Huey Attrill in his newspaper—was not right. For there was a board in the front yard of the small clapboard house that lay back between its two neighbours. To this was tacked a handbill that gave details of the sale just as they were published in the *Post-Despatch*. But angled across this notice was a strip of paper handwritten with the information that due to unforseen circumstances the sale was postponed until three o'clock this same afternoon.

'Hey, mister,' somebody called in a bored tone while Steele scowled at the notice of postponement and contemplated the prospect of having more than two hours to spare: which was a much longer time than he had ever needed to kill in this town before.

He looked back over his shoulder toward an open upper window of the house to the left of where Porter Calendar had lived. Saw a blonde, curly-haired girl of thirteen or so leaning out over the window sill, chewing with her mouth open as she idly tossed a balled-up wad of paper from one hand to the other.

'You want something, young lady?' he asked.

'Reckon not, mister,' she replied in the same monotone as before, the frown firmly fixed, marring her youthful prettiness. 'You want to know why they changed the time of the sale of old Calendar's junk?'

'No,' Steele told her, and had little difficulty in not fastening his gaze on the immature swells of the girl's breasts emphasised by the way she leaned out of the window so that the bodice of her dress was stretched tight.

'I'll tell you for fifty cents.'

'Thought you didn't want anything?'

'Everybody wants money. I can get by with a quarter.'

Steele pursed his lips, countered: 'I can get by without knowing why the sale start time was changed, kid.'

Boredom was replaced by irritability. She growled: 'All right then, a dime.'

'It doesn't even mean that much to me,' Steele replied as he made to start the pair of horses forward. But he held them back when the girl spat whatever she was chewing forcefully down into the street, clutched the wadded-up paper in both hands then shrugged her skinny shoulders, snarled sourly:

'So the hell with it! Mrs Jackson, that's the sister of Calendar who kicked the bucket so they had to sell his stuff, she showed up in town last night. And this mornin' at the Lakeview Hotel, she kicked the bucket, too. They had to telegraph Mr Jackson, her old man, ask him what to do. Holdin' off the sale while they wait for his answer. Maybe he'll wire back there ain't to be a sale. Hell of a thing, uh?'

'Sure is.'

'But ain't worth no money?'

'Not to me.'

'You can't blame a person for tryin', though?'

'I'm not blaming you for anything.'

She peered pointedly to left and right, obviously about to say something she did not want overheard. Then she asked in a rasping wisper: 'Hey, mister, what would you say to a little fuck?'

Steele took a moment to be sure his voice would sound

normal before he said: 'How old are you, young lady?'

'I'm eighteen.'

'So you don't only talk dirty?'

'What?'

'You tell lies, too.'

She snarled: 'I am eighteen, damnit. It's just I'm kinda real small for my age. So, mister: what do you say to a little fuck?'

Steele fixed her with a bleak-eyed gaze, touched the brim of his hat with a gloved forefinger, flicked the reins to start the horses moving. Raised his voice to be heard above the clop of hooves, the creak of turning wheels, answered evenly: 'Goodbye, little fuck.'

4

This was the first time he got at first hand indisputable evidence Front Street was not the only section of Broadwater where women could be bought: and as he drove away from one house where a furniture sale would maybe take place and another where an underaged girl was definitely available at a price, he guessed it was unlikely she was unique.

Then he put the girl child, the subject of women in general and much else out of his mind as he purposely made a left turn, headed toward Front Street. Came up in quick time with a plan of action.

First he would eat in some place that was not fancy and so could not justify charging fancy prices. Then find the premises of Rufus Grimes, the auctioneer and land agent handling the Calendar business: confirm whether or not the next-of-kin of the hapless brother and sister had given the go ahead for the sale to proceed.

Beyond this... Well, depending upon the length of time left to kill, he maybe just might try his luck somewhere a man with a few spare dollars in his pocket could increase his roll—or lose it.

He had planned nothing more concrete than this when he reached the intersection of the side street with Front: the mirror-smooth, sun-glinting, fresh-smelling lake spread out before him, a bank on one corner, a boarding house across from this.

From up the street to his right, where it curved out of sight beyond the bank, following the east shore contours of the lake, there came the jangling music of an out-of-tune piano

41

mixed in with raucous talk and gusts of false sounding laughter. To his left, across from where a family group picnicked on the sandy beach of the lake, he spotted the jutting sign of a livery stable. The sometimes shrill but less than strident talk and laughter of the parents and three young children on the beach were the most unobtrusive sounds from this direction and Steele steered the wagon to the left.

Called himself a weak-willed fool for turning his back on the area where Broadwater's well-known action was starting. But then discovered, when he had turned the rig over to the wizened old liveryman who was disgruntled that the horses needed just to be rested and the wagon was simply to be stored for awhile, he had to head north anyway. For at this end of the street, apart from the boarding house and the livery, there was only the Baptist chapel, a couple of shuttered, out-of-business stores and three that were open.

The closest restaurant, the sour-tempered liveryman told him, was three blocks north. He claimed not to know where Rufus Grimes did business. Then he looked like he was going to say something about the Colt Hartford rifle Steele took from under the wagon seat and sloped to his right shoulder. But he didn't: instead compressed his lips and wrinkled his eyes in a manner that suggested he knew something Steele should also know but he was damned if he was going to tell the cheapskate stranger—who did not want his horses curried or his wagon axles greased—what it was.

It was a perfect day to take a lakeside stroll, work up an appetite: if a man got any kind of pleasures in walking exercise for its own sake, or enjoyed panoramic views of fine scenery. Steele was not such a man. Even on the Trail's End spread amid the grandeur of the Providence River Valley, he preferred to ride. Survey the land he had made his own by right of possession purely in terms of the rolling acres being his own property rather than to wonder at its intrinsic, God-created beauty.

Here in Broadwater, as he ambled along the sidewalks, stepped down to cross the intersections, up on the other sides, he gave scant consideration to the glistening lake, the green-

42

timbered hillsides on the far shore. Instead, he consciously allowed his five senses free rein to assimilate in his mind the sights and sounds of the places he passed. Aware that these melded to stir his imagination, charge him with a once familiar brand of excitement. While, conversely, he was strongly aware of a degree of pleasure that he could enjoy these sensations without the need to work too hard at ignoring the tempting impulses they triggered.

He found a clean, ten-table restaurant on the north corner of Front and Fourth Streets. The blackboard bill of fare propped up outside offered plain food at reasonable prices, along with all the coffee a patron could drink at no extra charge. The old couple who ran it were the kind who liked to talk, and because Steele was their only customer they did a great deal of talking to him. The man behind the counter about the old days when Broadwater was a frontier town: better than any he had ever been in, be they cattle, army, timber, railroad or other gold towns. His wife, cooking up ham and eggs and grits for Steele in the kitchen, kept yelling through a hatch in the wall: to correct him in matters of fact, or disagree with his every opinion.

The food was greasy, the cutlery could have been cleaner, and one cup of weak coffee was enough for Steele. But for twenty-five cents the meal was filling. And the man was able to tell him that Rufus Grimes had an office up past the Blue Moon Saloon. His wife insisted that the auctioneer's office was this side of the most famous place of entertainment in Broadwater. But that it was on Front Street they were both in agreement.

It was after one o'clock now and the town had completely lost the quality of lethargy, at least along the mid-town stretch of Front Street. Where pianos, trumpets, guitars and fiddles played in tune or in discord with other music from neighbouring establishments. Barkers yelled at the passers by crowding the sidewalks, urging them to step inside and sample the untold delights on offer. Customers shouted for drinks, shrieked delight when gambles paid off, groaned when they lost. And even the brightly painted signs seemed to

43

come to noisy life, so garish were their appeals above store fronts, saloons, eating houses and, causing Steele to do a double-take, an evangelical church.

Most of the people on this side of the street were men, just a few of them with eager young women clinging to their arms. On the lakeside, dotted along the curves of the beach, were family groups, courting couples or elderly ladies in pairs or small groups.

There was a bustling to-ing and fro-ing of wagons and horseback riders along Front Street.

More men carried guns that did not. But with the exception of Adam Steele all of those not riding a horse or wagon packed just holstered revolvers. And a number of quizzical glances were directed at the Virginian as he sauntered along the busy street, the unusual, revolver action sporting rifle sloped to his shoulder. He ignored this mild degree of interest shown in him: concentrated upon looking for a shingle that would show that Rufus Grimes had an office up on the second or third story of one of the buildings he passed.

Then he sensed that somebody had a keener interest in him: knew a pair of eyes gazed fixedly at him. But he failed to meet these eyes of the man he soon realised was following him. A tall, broad-shouldered, loose-limbed, neatly-dressed man who remained a constant twenty or so paces behind the Virginian.

When he had made absolutely sure that the man was trailing him—paused on every occasion he stopped to pretend to study store windows—Steele began to plan how he would satisfy his curiosity about him. This would entail turning on to the next outside stairway he came to, entering what he hoped would be a quiet office where he could get the drop on the man, ask him what the hell he wanted.

But then Steele saw something that caused him to forget about his tail. This was the dilapidated wagon he had seen twice before: at the funeral of Arlene Forrester and at the night camp beside the trail between Providence and the Timber Creek spur to his spread.

This afternoon Esteban Garcia was neither up on the seat

nor in sight anywhere nearby. But his two diminutive daughters were squatted in the rear of the wagon: hunkered down in attitudes that suggested they they were guarding their father's blade sharpening equipment set up, ready to be operated, on the wagon bed.

But, Steele abruptly sensed, there was something wrong. For as he drew closer it was plain to see that Conchita and Maria Garcia were afraid. They were rigid with tension as they stared intently at the building out front of which the wagon was parked. Which was the Blue Moon Saloon, large enough to spread the entire length of a block between Sixth and Seventh Streets.

The façade behind the balcony-shaded sidewalk was featured with several doors under signs that named what lay beyond and Garcia had stopped the wagon outside, plainly had entered, the double doorway with decorated glass panels under the legend that proclaimed: BLUE MOON SALOON: MAIN ENTRANCE.

Just for a moment as he started to lengthen his stride along the crowded sidewalk in front of the massive brick and timber building, did Steele consider the possibility the Mexican had taken the facetious advice offered at the Providence cemetery. But a moment later the futile notion was gone. For he was close enough to recognise that the two young girls were not merely anxious about the lengthy absense of their father. They could see something through the patterned glass panels of the two doors that terrified them.

Then they sprang to their feet, shouted their fear to each other.

Steele was within a dozen paces of the rear of the wagon. Used his free hand to shove disgruntled people out of his path.

Conchita snapped her head around to look away from the younger sister, back at the doorway, caught sight of and recognised Steele: glowered fixedly at him for a second, showed she still felt nothing good toward him.

'*Conchita, una ojeada——*' Maria shouted, jerked up an arm to point a shaking finger across the sidewalk at the building entrance.

The double doors crashed violently open. Passers by scattered, vented curses and screams. And something was flung outside: a man. Esteban Garcia, his arms and legs flailing as he struggled to break his fall. But he hit the sidewalk with a sickening thud, slid across the boards, crashed down on the street beneath his wagon.

A stream of curses were snarled out of the doorway. The Mexican's sombrero was scaled in his wake. The two girls shrieked in their own language. Garcia added his voice to the cacophony of sound. And all the noise spooked the burros. But luckily for the man under the wagon, the brakes were hard on and the pair of animals were able to drag the rig only a short way. So he was spared the danger of getting hit by a skidding wheelrim.

Maria plunged down to the sidewalk, did not try to prevent herself falling: then turned and rolled fast on to the street, weeping her concern for her father as she struggled to pull him out from under the rig. While her older sister leapt off the wagon, snatched up the sombrero, clutched it to her, began to direct a stream of Mexican Spanish through the wide open doorway.

Maybe he understood what was said. Or guessed the substance from the girls' malevolent expression and shrill tone of voice. Whatever, the man who had thrown Garcia out of the Blue Moon was incensed by the sight and sound of the slightly built, four feet high Mexican girl. And he took a long stride over the threshold, his right arm swinging, hand splayed, to launch a powerful blow at Conchita's head.

'*Señor*, she does not know what she is——' Garcia shrieked. Dragged himself out from under the rear of the wagon, Maria clutched to his side as they both stared in horror at the tableau on the sidewalk.

Steele registered the hurried impression of a heavyset man with white hair and a pale face, a vivid red patch at the centre of the cheek he could see. A head taller than his own five and a half feet height, maybe weighing half as much again as he did: but whether he was overweight with fat or had a heavily muscled frame, the Virginian had no time to take account of.

46

He snapped the rifle down from his shoulder, took a two handed grip on the frame and swung it across a sideways arc, like a club.

At the last moment the man intent upon landing a vicious blow against the small girl saw something that streaked toward his head. And he checked his swinging arm, turned his glowering face to Steele. The Virginian saw the matching red smudge of deep anger on the other cheek as the thick lips of the enraged man broke apart, about to vent a shriek his glittering eyes warned would be an ugly obscenity.

But before he could utter a sound the barrel of the Colt Hartford crashed into his Adam's apple. He had already halted in his tracks, half turned toward Steele, no longer bothered by the tiny child who stood, scowlingly defiant and now silent before him. And the impact of the rifle barrel against his throat sent him staggering backwards out of an instant of inertia, along the threshold of the saloon, so that he slammed into the doorframe.

Where he teetered for a moment, eyes rolled up into their lids, before he started to slide slowly down, to end in a seated attitude, legs splayed and arms limp at his sides. Hovered on the brink of unconsciousness as he made choking sounds that suggested he was fighting the threat of nausea: desperately tried not to vomit on his crisply clean shirt, vest and pants.

The chorus of raucous sounds that exploded in the wake of Garcia's ejection from the Blue Moon Saloon had been followed by a short, tense silence when the big, white-haired man stepped out on the sidewalk, launched the swipe toward the small girl standing helplessly before him. Then another body of vocal sound, largely approving, Steele had fleetingly thought, erupted as the Virginian violently stopped the blow being landed. This faltered and faded as the big man was reduced to helplessness himself, slid down the doorway, and Steele dropped a hand away from the Colt Hartford, sloped the rifle to his shoulder again. But it did not end completely until Esteban Garcia blurted:

'Behind you, *señor*!'

And Steele felt the unmistakable pressure of a gun muzzle

pressed forcefully against the small of his shirt-covered back. When he held perfectly still, sweating from every pore, while he stared fixedly at the suffering big man seated in the doorway.

Conchita spun suddenly around, rushed into one comforting arm of her father while his other arm continued to clasp Maria close to him. And all three Mexicans peered at Steele, their big dark eyes articulate with tacit gratitude: but with shock and fear lurking just in back of this. Then the man who held the gun against Steele's spine asked without rancour:

'You have it in mind to do anythin' else to Whitney Burnett now he's down and almost out, stranger?'

'Reckon it's already enough to keep him from beating up on the child, feller,' the Virginian replied in the same tone, abruptly easier in his mind about this man who had the drop on him.

'More than enough to get yourself in a whole lot of trouble, I figure.'

'*Señor, Sheriff! El grande hombre* . . . He was about to——'

'Just a deputy, Mex,' the man behind Steele broke in, confirmed what the Virginian had guessed after Garcia addressed him with a title. He had spoken with Broadwater's senior peace officer in the past and this man didn't sound anything like Sheriff Gavin Fenton.

Steele looked over the shoulder that did not have the rifle sloped to it, saw the deputy was the man he had spotted tailing him. He had unfastened his suit jacket, to draw the revolver from his hip holster. And this revealed the star pinned to his shirt.

'Yeah, I'm the one was watchin' you, stranger,' the deputy confirmed when he read recognition in the Virginian's gaze. 'On account of it seemed to me a man who totes a rifle the way you do, he's lookin' for trouble.'

The crowd had started to disperse, buzzing with talk again. And the interrupted noise from within the Blue Moon Saloon and off the beach across the street had recommenced. Broadwater had a reputation for being a law abiding town. It was taken for granted that now the law was on the scene of the trouble, the trouble was over.

'I don't carry a revolver,' Steele replied. 'Rifle's to take care of trouble that's already started. If it concerns me. Or people I know.'

'Okay, I saw what happened,' the deputy allowed. 'If Burnett had connected he'd likely have broke the kid's neck. So I figure you did him a favour. Kept him out of jail. Saved the court time and money for tryin' and hangin' him, too.'

'Hell, Dexter, you can't hang somebody for killin' a Mexican!' a man yelled out through the open doorway.

Steele looked inside, saw a group of ten hard-looking men, half as many painted-up women, all of them expensively attired, in the elegantly furnished lobby of the Blue Moon. All the men expressed mean grins that suggested that any one of them might have voiced the racist opinion. Then a redheaded woman with a spectacularly curved body taunted:

'Let's hope that snotnosed kid's old man has learned his lesson good enough without no killin', Dexter! His kind just don't march in the front door of a place like the Blue Moon and start askin' their damn questions. Next time he'll go round the back, not cause no trouble!'

'You folks quit flappin' your jaws!' the deputy snarled. 'And somebody best go bring a sawbones to take a look at Whitney Burnett. Make sure he ain't damaged more serious than he looks.' He pressed the gun a fraction harder into Steele's spine, growled: 'And unless you like livin' dangerously, stranger, be best you get outta Broadwater before Whitney's restored to full health—and strength!'

'Grateful for the advice,' Steele said. 'But I've got some unfinished business to attend to before I leave.'

'It just better be business that don't mean trouble for anybody, Mr...?'

'Steele, feller.'

'Hey, the guy who moved in on the old Sanderson place down in the valley?' Dexter asked, surprised.

'Right.'

'We heard about you, Steele. You sure do manage to get yourself mixed up in some bad trouble now and then.'

'I've already told you I don't go looking for it. So, no. My business in Broadwater doesn't mean trouble for anybody.

49

I'm not like you, feller.'

'What's that supposed to mean?' the lawman growled, ready to get angry. And he pressed the gun muzzle even harder into Steele's back, like he was intent upon forcefully prodding an answer out of the Virginian.

Steele wriggled his spine against the muzzle, drawled: 'I've got nothing against anybody.'

5

Esteban Garcia attempted to thank Steele effusively for what
he had done to save Conchita from injury. But he was cut
short by Dexter. Who removed the gun from its threat
against Steele and repeated his warning to the Mexican.
Expanded on it: told him to leave Broadwater before Burnett
or Burnett's friends took it into their heads to even the score
for the trouble Garcia could be said to have started.

This as two of the hard-looking men from the lobby of the
Blue Moon came forward to haul the hoarsely groaning
Burnett to his feet and help him back inside. While Garcia,
still with a scrawny arm around the narrow shoulders of each
of his daughters, peered beseechingly at Steele.

'I have to agree with the deputy, feller,' the Virginian said.

'But I went into the hotel only to ask about my wife,
Carmelita, *señor*!'

'And it's like it was in Providence,' Steele reminded. 'Only
worse, I reckon.'

'*Señor*, I do not——'

'If they're beating up on you, they sure won't be inclined to
tell you the truth, even if they talk to you.'

The double doors of the saloon slammed closed so hard
that the glass panels rattled in their frames.

'And maybe it won't get any better,' Steele added. 'So
maybe you should give up looking, head back to Mexico?'

'Shit, I—' Dexter was immediately disconcerted he had
unthinkingly blurted out the dirty word within earshot of the
pair of solemn-eyed little girls. Cleared his throat, found his
ill-humour fired up by embarrassment as he divided a scowl

between Steele and Garcia, complained: 'Hell, I don't neither know nor care why either of you guys are here. I'm not makin' no requests. And I don't give a damn whether you head south for Mexico, north, east or swim across the lousy lake to wherever! But I'm sure orderin' you to leave town before sundown. For your own good. And, Goddamnit, for the sake of upholdin' law here in Broadwater. So you two get the hell out: before sundown, okay? *Se comprende*? Understand?'

Dexter was a good looking, well built man of about thirty, with a burnished complexion that probably looked darker than it was because of his sandy hair. He looked a lot older when his lean features were hardened by his anger that was not directed entirely at the Virginian and the Mexican.

Steele acknowledged: 'Before that, if the furniture sale at the Calendar house isn't going to go ahead.'

'*Si, Diputado Sheriff*,' Garcia allowed miserably. '*Tiene razon. Mi amigo, Señor* Steele, he is right. Our search, it is *inutil...* useless to continue in the towns where to be Mexican is to be treated like a dog. Come, Maria, Conchita. *Adios, señor* Steele. *Muchas gracias.*'

He stooped to speak in a rasping whisper to his daughters. And they both recited their polite thanks and farewells in well-practised unison. Finished with less than elegant curtsies.

Then Maria allowed herself to be lifted and swung gently into the rear of the wagon while the older-than-her-years Conchita climbed aboard without help. As soon as the grim faced Garcia was up on the seat, the reins in his slightly shaking hands, he released the brakes and steered the wagon into a tight turn to head south. Which maybe, Steele thought, signified that the Mexican really was going back to Baja California.

The lawman, less tense now, asked of the Virginian: 'That sale that interests you, mister? The one being handled by Rufus Grimes?'

'That's right. Looking for Grimes to see if the sale's going ahead. I heard there's doubt about it.'

'Yeah, that's right. On account of Calendar's sister dropped

52

dead too. You'll most likely find Rufus in the Red Dog Saloon—that's up on the corner of Tenth Street—this time of day. Or if he's already finished his liquid lunch, he'll probably be in his office, above the Commercial Bank that's next to the saloon.'

'I'm grateful.'

'Some advice for you, Steele.'

'I take it sometimes.'

'Don't play any cards with the bunch of innocent lookin' old-timers who run a game in the Red Dog most all day long.'

'They cheat?'

Dexter shook his head emphatically. 'No, it ain't that. Sharps don't last as long as that bunch in this town. It's just they ain't so green as they try to make out.'

'I'm grateful again.'

The lawman showed a brief smile with a hint of cruel relish in the glinting light of his pale blue eyes, said in a low pitched voice: 'And I appreciated seein' Whitney Burnett laid out the way he was... Especially the way he was.' He laughed, fingered his throat, muttered: 'Now that sonofabitch has got the pain in the neck he always is to other folks around here.' He turned away, raised a hand, looked back and added: 'Don't let me see you in town after sundown, you hear.'

Steele found Grimes—a dapper little man with bright eyes, a pouting mouth, jet black hair, sidewhiskers and eyebrows that met in the middle—at the first place Dexter had predicted: drinking beer in the Red Dog Saloon. A bar that was a lot less plush than what the Virginian had seen of the Blue Moon, but with a little more style than the Golden Gate back in Providence.

The auctioneer, who did his drinking standing up at the polished bar counter with the brass foot rail, reminded Steele somewhat of Harlan Grout: the way the man was obviously drunk but was in steady control to himself. Unlike the Providence liveryman, Grimes was a compulsive and fast talker: the kind of man who found it impossible to supply a simple answer to a straightforward question.

He told Steele that Calendar's brother-in-law—the hus-

53

band of the unfortunate woman who died so suddenly after making the long trip down to Broadwater from San Francisco—had wired that the sale should go ahead as planned. So three o'clock was indeed the time to be at number sixty five California Avenue. Where it looked, Grimes complained, like the rancher from the Providence River Valley might have the pick of the lots at the rock bottom reserve prices. For announcements of the forthcoming sale in several local newspapers had not exactly set this part of the country alight with interest.

With the promise of a ride to the sale in Rufus Grimes' buggy, Steele had better than an hour to kill. So, forearmed with advice from the deputy sheriff, he accepted an invitation to take a chair in the five-handed game of five card stud poker at a corner table of the Red Dog Saloon. But first he had to buy a draught of beer he had no intention of drinking: this to placate the scowling bartender who told him in snarling tones the Red Dog was not in the business of selling coffee to non-drinkers who had no damn business using the comforts and facilities of his establishment. Which was a point Steele understood.

No limit was set by the middle-aged to elderly card players who looked to the Virginian like full time professional gamblers who were down on their luck: playing low ante games while they waited for the first signs that a winning streak was being generated. None of them ever raised by more than two dollars, so Steele went along with this. Knew he was ahead by more than thirty dollars when Grimes showed at the batwing doors and said it was time to leave for the sale.

Steele had a three dollar investment in the latest pot and held a full house, aces and kings, against two players who were eager to bet.

'Fold,' he said, tossed in his hand. 'Enjoyed the game and the pleasure of your company, gentlemen.'

'But you can't leave yet!'

'You gotta——'

Steele rose from the table, picked up the rifle that had been leaning against his chair and sloped it to his shoulder. His bright smile gave no hint that he knew he was supposed to be a patsy as he collected his money off the table with his free hand.

The four men still seated at the table made no attempt to conceal their disaffection with this stranger who left the game so abruptly, without giving them a chance to get back the money they had allowed him to win. And the gazes that were fastened on him as he left the Red Dog Saloon seemed to have palpable force: his back felt like it was being bombarded with pinpricks until the batwing doors flapped closed behind him.

So although it had not been the kind of high stakes poker Steele would have preferred to play in Broadwater, the game had generated a different brand of tension that had served to pass the time pleasantly enough. While it allowed him the opportunity to divide his concentration between his cards, the other players and the doorway: this last to check on the new customers who entered the saloon. But if any friends of Whitney Burnett came into the Red Dog they kept an extremely discreet watch on him.

The anxiously frowning Grimes drove his smart new buggy along Tenth Street then made a right on to the virtually traffic-free California Avenue: rather than headed south on the much busier Front Street. Which was fine with Steele, who quickly came to realise that the city-suited auctioneer was as garrulous as the couple at the restaurant where he ate lunch. But his line of talk had purpose. He prattled about the fine quality of the furniture and other household effects that were to come under his hammer at the Calendar home: and how sadly unfortunate it would be if the new widower, Ezra Jackson, failed to get reasonable prices for the items in the immediate wake of the double tragedy that had struck his family.

Steele sat silently beside the talkative little man and paid only scant attention to the less than subtle attempts to win his sympathy. Rested the Colt Hartford across his knees and gripped it in both gloved hands. Kept constant watch on the houses along each side of California, the corners of the intersecting streets and the fences, walls and plantings that could provide hiding places from which an ambush might be sprung. He also scrutinised windows from which it would be easy for a bushwhacker to fire a shot.

But he thought it unlikely that, if revenge was in anyone's mind, it would be so swift. Or so crude. In daylight, on the streets of Broadwater which was such a law-abiding town under the jurisdiction of Sheriff Gavin Fenton and his team of tough, reputedly honest, deputies.

And so it proved. For they reached their destination without incident and only then, as the buggy rolled to a halt outside the house that lay back between its neighbours, did Steele sense watching eyes. First saw a small knot of a half dozen women and two elderly men gathered in the front yard of the Calendar house. But they looked with just mild, slightly resentful interest at the two men who stepped down from the buggy. Hostility, singled out for Steele, was directed down by the pretty blonde-haired young girl who leaned out from the same window as earlier. Glowered at the Virginian with eyes that wished every kind of evil upon him.

Then she taunted bitterly as Grimes bustled on ahead of Steele: 'I hope you get beaten outta every damn thing you want, smartass!'

Some of the women snorted their disapproval.

Steele winked at the girl, answered: 'And I hope before you get any worse, you get your ass beaten by your Pa.'

The girl poked out her tongue and slammed the window closed against a buzz of shocked talk from the group in the yard of the next door house. Then a particularly sour faced woman of fifty or so shook her head, raised her voice to tell Steele:

'Howard Falls has tried everythin' to tame that no account daughter of his, mister. Includin' paddlin' her hindquarters. But I reckon she's too far gone beyond redemption for anythin' to work with her. And the way I see it, it don't do the girl no good at all to bad-talk back to her the same kinda way she bad-talks to you!'

Grimes used a key to unlock the door of the Calendar

house as one of the old men, who needed two sticks to walk with, held back, turned to leer at Steele, rasped softly through crooked, discoloured teeth:

'Sounds like you and that Dolly Falls already had words, am I right?'

'Yeah, feller, dirty ones,' Steele answered as the rest of the group pressed forward, eager to follow the dapper little auctioneer into the dead man's house.

The lame old-timer licked twitching lips, dribbled some saliva down his bristled chin, his red-rimmed eyes blinking rapidly. Then he swallowed hard, asked in a thick-toned voice: 'She happen to give you a peek at them buds she got down the front of her dress, mister? She does that sometimes. Brazen little tease. And other times, she'll show the tops of her legs that way——'

He was somewhat deaf, and like many hard of hearing people his voice was louder than he thought. He broke off and grimaced when the sour faced woman yelled from in the house:

'You're nothin' else but a dirty old man, Crabtree!'

Crabtree, who looked to be well past eighty, glowered through the doorway, said to Steele: 'Ain't nothin' dirty about it, seems to me. Only natural a man would want to get inside the drawers of such a cute lookin' little lady. And his age sure ain't got nothin' to do with it, ain't that so, mister?'

The window of the Falls house crashed open again. And the girl yelled down at the two men who had moved out of her line of vision into the dead man's front yard: 'You got no Goddamn chance, Fulton Crabtree! Why the hell I want you inside my drawers, uh? When I already got one asshole in there?'

57

6

This latest profanity triggered another wave of vocal shock from the elderly ladies inside the house of Broadwater's late druggist. But the gasps and breathless remarks quickly faltered as interest in the impending sale became of greater importance than the off-colour language and shameful behaviour of Dolly Falls.

With the door closed and six women and four men crowded into the house, the rooms probably seemed more cramped than they actually were. Steele kept colliding with people, sometimes accidentally knocked them with the Colt Hartford. He soon gave up muttering apologies for this, though, when the words drew only glowering glares in response as he moved about the two floors of the small house. In which, it looked like, little appeared to have changed since Porter S. Calendar lived there: except that every item of furniture now had a numbered card thumb tacked to it.

When he had carefully viewed all the items in the sale, Steele had just one query for Rufus Grimes. Was told by the impatient auctioneer that any piece of furniture in which anything was stored included the articles inside. But, eager as he obviously was to get the sale started, the loquacious Grimes could not leave it there, assured the Virginian he had little to be concerned about in terms of competing bids from the majority of the other people in the house.

'They're mostly regular attenders at this kind of event,' Grimes said in the kind of stage whisper that served as token attempt at confidentiality but was loud enough for his remarks to carry to others. But they all seemed too thick-skinned to take his criticism to heart. 'Some of them are nothing more than nosey parkers. I'm sure they'd make a tour of every house in town if it was all right to do so before the owners were dead. Others will simply buy up anything dirt cheap they think they'll be able to hock at Charlie Kennedy's pawnshop for whatever few cents profit they can get.'

Steele turned away from the auctioneer before he had chance to launch into an extended version of the low opinion he held of his fellow townspeople at the sale. And the suspicion he was again being set up, as in the card game at the Red Dog Saloon, got stronger by the moment as he reflected on much of what Grimes had said. This while he double checked the items for which he intended to bid, formed his decisions.

Grimes took his timing from when the Virginian was through viewing: commenced the sale in the parlour. He was no beginner in the auctioneering business. Even faced with such a small group of laymen, bargain hunting among the mundane personal effects of a small-town druggist who had owned nothing of great beauty or value, the dapper little man treated the sale professionally. Encouraged and accepted bids with fast, smooth talk. Knocked down the items sold with a sharp rap of the brass gavel in his right hand against a much beaten circle of wood in the palm of his left.

For most of the time his sidewhiskered face was impassive as the small eyes below his connected eyebrows moved over the audience.

In the parlour there were two lots of interest to Steele: a walnut writing bureau and a pair of glass-fronted oak bookcases containing some volumes on medical subjects—as befitted a druggist—but many more that were works of fiction.

He bought the bookcases and contents at the reasonable reserve placed on them by Grimes. Then ignored all the other lots sold at giveaway prices to various Broadwater citizens, until the bureau came up. But he dropped out of the bidding for this when it reached fifteen dollars: gave no indication that he saw Grimes' inscrutability crack and the auctioneer exchange a disconcerted glance with the sour faced women he had heard called Mrs Bonney.

In the kitchen it was the same woman who once again competed with him for a storage cabinet that was virtually worthless but was packed with good quality pots and pans and china. This time the bidding halted at ten dollars fifty, after Steele dropped out at ten. And Mrs Bonney and Grimes were again disturbed at how this part of the sale turned out.

Upstairs there was a wardrobe that had captured Steele's attention, even though he was not interested in the clothes inside: they were for a man much taller and broader than he. On this occasion it was the old-timer without need of sticks who was as eager as Steele to buy: and at nine dollars, after a flurry of fifty cents bidding, Steele called a halt for a different reason than before. He was convinced that his competitor, who was as tall and broadly built as Calendar had obviously been, genuinely wanted the clothes in the wardrobe.

He was then able to purchase two ceramic-based kerosene lamps, a crate of carpentry tools and four watercolour seascapes without competition: even persuaded Grimes to reduce the reserves on the pictures.

There were still some lots to sell off after Steele had secured most of the items he wanted, missed out on the bureau, the collection of kitchen and eating utensils and the wardrobe. But he felt reasonably content with the result of his visit to Broadwater as he headed down Second Street to Front, rounded the corner toward the livery to pick up his wagon and team.

It was close to five o'clock now and the sky had clouded over to blot out the sinking sun. Already a number of the brasher places of entertainment lining the lakeside had brightly lighted windows and some had lit outside lamps to illuminate their signs. A chill evening breeze was blowing in off Providence Lake and the beach was now deserted for as far as he could see along it.

The ill-tempered liveryman who was laying a fire in a stove in a corner of the stable greeted Steele without niceties. Said he had heard how a man who looked a lot like the Virginian got involved in some trouble over a Mexican family up at the Blue Moon Saloon.

'It was nothing serious, feller,' Steele told the leather-aproned old man with a battered hat on the back of his almost bald head, began to hitch the two horses into the wagon traces.

'Maybe it wasn't so much to you at the time, mister. But I hear Whitey Burnett took it kinda hard.'

'What I heard of it,' Steele said as he continued to concentrate his attention on harnessing the team to the wagon, 'Burnett should be grateful I kept him from killing a little kid.'

The liveryman cackled with laughter, saliva bubbling in his throat. 'Hell, killin' a Mex brat wouldn't mean so much around this neck of the woods! Luke Dexter, he only said that to keep up appearances, is my guess. But it wasn't all bullshit that new deputy give you, mister. Best you take the advice I hear he handed out to you. On account of after sundown there are a whole lot of real dark places in Broadwater where a man can come to harm. And no lawman to see it. A big, deep lake out there where a body weighed down with some rocks ain't never likely to be found.'

He laughed wetly again, worked the spit into his mouth and directed it in a long, dark coloured stream at the floor. Then was abruptly afraid, backed off from Steele as the Virginian jerked up from checking the tension of the harness: snapped his head around. But ignored the liveryman, to look toward the doorway where he had heard a sound.

One of the men from the card game at the Red Dog Saloon, named Buddy as he recalled, stepped in through the part open doorway, said evenly: 'Like John York there, mister, we heard about how you riled up Burnett. Who's a real mean bastard to get on the wrong side of. So we're real glad we met up with you again before him and his Blue Moon friends did. Left nothin' much of you for us to meet up with.'

Both doors folded open wider and two more of the Red Dog men stepped into view, one at each side of the first to show.

'When Buddy talks about *we*, he means all four of us, Steele,' the one on the left said. His name was Phil.

Jacko, on the right, confirmed: 'Yeah, all of us you run out on before we planned for the game to finish.'

The fourth man, Billy, edged into the livery a little nervously, but tried his best to hide his fear, although he could not meet Steele's level gaze.

All of them were middle-aged to elderly, but none was frail and they out-numbered the Virginian four to one. As they slowly advanced in a line into the livery, their footfalls were light, so York's giggling laughter from the rear corner of the malodorous stable was the loudest sound. Steele saw no visible guns, or signs of concealed weapons. Thought for a moment as he stood in front of the horses harnessed to the wagon, the Colt Hartford out of his reach under the seat, about Dexter's claim that card sharps did not stay long in Broadwater. Wondered if this meant it was unnecessary for local gambling men to pack guns: whether cheats got themselves shot or were run out of town.

'This guy rub you Red Dog boys up the wrong way, too?' York asked eagerly. 'Cheat on you at cards?'

The line of shabbily dressed men came to a shuffling halt some six feet in front of Steele. All of them now wore matched expressions of grim resolution: for Billy evidently had drawn courage from being close to the others. The spade-bearded Buddy, who had been the least talkative during the poker game, was elected spokesman now.

He made a fist of his right hand, twisted the knuckles back and forth in the cupped palm of the left, fixed Steele with a hard gaze, but spoke in response to the liveryman: 'If you weren't such an addle-brained crazy old sonofabitch, York, you'd know better than to ask a question like that. Us boys find a man cheatin' in our game, he don't even get far as the swingin' doors of the Red Dog. Let alone have the time to shop for furniture before we stroll down the street and find him.'

He spat out the side of his mouth toward York. Moderated his tone, said to Steele: 'We figure you took us for thirty bucks, give or take a couple of cents. We'll settle for the round thirty, okay?'

Steele countered evenly: 'You just told the liveryman here I didn't cheat, so how is it I *took* you fellers?'

'Hell, we let you win, that's how!' the youngest, previously most uneasy member of the quartet growled, button eyes gleaming with righteous indignation.

'Shuddup, Billy!' the bespectacled Phil snapped. 'We agreed we'd let Buddy do the yakkin', didn't we?'

Buddy nodded his satisfaction with this, explained to the Virginian: 'We saw you talkin' with that Grimes guy, Steele. But we didn't know you was goin' to one of his auction sales. Figured you for a gamblin' man lookin' for a game and——'

'What I am, what I was right there at the Red Dog,' Steele cut in.

'Uh?' Buddy did not like to be interrupted with a correction, scowled his irritation.

'I gamble, feller. And I was looking for a game.'

Buddy nodded his satisfaction again. More emphatically, like he considered he had been proved right against the odds. 'What it seemed to us. And so we figured you'd stick around, enjoy the game for longer than you did.'

'Yeah, somebody told me you might plan on me doing that.'

'What's he mean, Buddy?' Billy wanted to know. 'What d'you mean, Steele? Who told you what about us, uh?'

York supplied eagerly: 'It was one of them two new deputies Gavin Fenton hired on last month! Name of Luke Dexter. It was Dexter took a hand in the trouble with Whitey and that greaser family and this guy. Outside the Blue Moon.'

'Shit, what's Gavin Fenton want with more help, damnit?' the narrow-faced, slit-eyed Jacko complained bitterly. 'Soon there'll be so much law in the streets of Broadwater nobody'll be to spit in the damn lake! Mark my words, the more friggin' lawmen there are, the more friggin' laws they make for the sonsofbitches to enforce! The sheriff and just them two sidekicks he used to have backin' him was enough law around here, seems to me!'

Buddy spread a pensive frown across his bearded face during this exchange, then showed a sly grin, announced: 'Well, it seems to me Steele; since you been told the way we work—not cheat, hear, work—then you was kinda cheatin' on us. To have us let you win, then walk away before we were ready for the game to end. So, thirty dollars, mister. Best you hand it over. Me and Billy, Phil and Jacko, we'll divvy it up amongst us later.'

Steele said: 'And if I say I don't recall any time limits set on the game?'

'Hell, that don't have nothin' to do with it!' Buddy argued, allowing his anger to show itself in a harsher tone, a faster twisting of one fisted hand in the palm of the other. 'An honest gambler don't just get up and walk out on a game without givin' the other players a chance to win back what they lost!'

'As I understand it,' Steele said with a slight shrug, 'you fellers wanted me to win.'

'Damnit, you know that was just a——' Billy started.

'Stay quiet, Billy,' Buddy broke in evenly, getting a grip on his anger again. He kept his hands together, but stopped the twisting action as he eyed Steele quizzically, asked: 'Well?'

'If I tell you to go to hell?' the Virginian countered flatly.

Billy was nervous again, had trouble remaining silent as sweat broke out on his brow despite the chill breeze that flowed in through the open doorway of the livery.

'We take it off you,' Buddy said with low-toned menace. 'The hard way. Plus some interest. That we take outta your hide.'

'Go to hell,' Steele challenged. Raised his left hand to scratch at his throat above the grey silken kerchief draped around his neck.

Billy may have hoped, but none of them had really expected it to be as easy as asking for their money back and getting it. So they had prepared a plan to get what they wanted the hard way.

Buddy grunted, took a step toward Steele. Pulled his hands apart, kept the right one clenched in a fist, the left cupped. A moment later lunged forward with a rasping exhalation of his breath. Began to throw a punch and made to fasten a grip on his victim's shirt front.

But Steele did not do as expected. He should have tried to back off from Buddy, been denied this line of escape by the horses he had just put in the wagon traces. Maybe gone to left or right, to be blocked by the other three Red Dog men.

Instead, he launched himself forward, his move much faster than Buddy's. He also had the element of surprise on his side, which suddenly expanded as he wrenched his hand away from his throat in a blur of speed: fixed around a weighted corner of his kerchief. The diagonally opposite corner likewise had a lead weight sewn into it. So as the scarf circled around the back of Buddy's neck, momentum carried it through a full circle. Then Steele brought up his free hand, streaked it under the left forearm, caught the flying corner. And when he pushed his right hand to the far left, his left to the right, the fabric noose tightened around Buddy's neck.

The man's surprise suddenly became bug-eyed, gaping-mouthed terror. And he realised that within less than two seconds of launching his attack against Steele, he was in danger of being throttled. And his mouth gaped wider in a silent scream while his eyes flicked rapidly to right and left as he searched for help. He tried to hook clawed fingers over the fabric that bit deep into his flesh.

Steele glanced around as his horses snorted and shied their nervousness. He saw the other three men from the Red Dog were some feet away, held in frozen attitudes of shock: also glimpsed John York on the out of focus periphery of his vision. The old liveryman was cursing as he fumbled to take down a shotgun off a rack on the wall near the stove.

'Thirty bucks doesn't seem so much to die for!' Steele rasped. Peered into Buddy's face at short range. Recognised the man was on the brink of passing out as his hands abandoned the struggle to hook over the scarf and his arms fell limply to his sides.

The Virginian eased the tension of his crossed-over arms a fraction and Buddy sank to his knees: stale, pent-up breath rasping out through his now gritted teeth.

'Stand aside, you guys!'

The bellowed command drew all attention toward John York. Who had freed the double barrel shotgun from its wall rack. And now he aimed it from his skinny right hip, hands shaking, thumb fumbling to draw back both hammers.

'You don't let go of Buddy Benson, stranger, I'll blast you from here to Kingdom Come!' he snarled.

Steele shifted his unblinking gaze from York to Phil and Jacko as they started to back away from him on one side. Then he looked at Billy, who seemed to be rooted to the spot. Lastly he peered down into the upturned face of the man who knelt before him.

Now the horses had calmed there was a brittle silence within the stable and the Virginian spoke much more softly than had York when he said:

'If thirty bucks isn't worth this feller dying for, old-timer, I don't reckon it's worth you killing for. With that gun at this range, could be both of us.'

Billy suddenly swung around, started toward the livery-man snarled: 'Don't be a fool! Both of them, hell! You'll likely drop the whole bunch of us with that scatter gun!'

He kept his bulky body in front of the wavering weapon, then gripped the barrels with both hands, eased it out of York's grasp. Broke open the gun, turned, grimaced as he displayed the empty breeches, growled:

'Damn old scatter gun ain't even loaded.' He held it up toward the fading light that came in through the open doorway so he could peer down the insides of the barrels. Wrinkled his nose, added: 'Full of dust and ain't likely been fired in years I'd guess.'

York defended sullenly: 'Leastways I tried my best! Tried to keep the stranger from makin' suckers outta you Red Dog boys.'

Buddy made gurgling sounds.

Steele shifted his dark-eyed gaze from him to the pained man's three partners, said with a trace of contempt in his voice and expression: 'Even without talking with the new

66

deputy I'd have figured out I was being set up. Like I say, I'm a gambling man. Been one for a lot of years. Played in a lot of games all over the country. So I reckon I know most of the angles, most of the tricks.'

He released one corner of the scarf, drew it from around the neck of Buddy Benson. Who sank lower on his knees, until his rump rested on his heels. He brought up both hands, massaged the reddened area of his grizzled skin.

Billy asked: 'What the hell kinda trick bandana is that, mister?'

'The kind some Indians who aren't redskins use to kill people,' Steele answered cryptically, hung the thuggee scarf back around his own neck.

Then he moved alongside his horses to get within reach of the Colt Hartford stowed under the wagon seat. But it seemed the others were as drained of the will to continue the abortive fight as Benson by what had happened to the bearded man.

He climbed up on the seat, reached beneath it to bring the rifle into view, lay it across his knees. Held it there with one gloved hand as he unwound the reins with the other.

Billy tossed the still broken open shotgun into an empty stall with an expression that suggested it smelled bad: he even wiped the palms of his hands down the sides of his pants.

Benson let himself be helped to his feet by Phil and Jacko, then eyed Steele with scowling reproach as he growled huskily: 'That's a sneaky doodad you got there, mister. But if my partners had been packin' their guns you wouldn't have got away with any of this!'

Steele reminded him evenly: 'I said I like games of chance. In my opinion, thirty bucks isn't worth dying or killing for.'

'Yeah, you said both them,' Jacko muttered.

Steele nodded. 'I took a chance all of you fellers would agree with that opinion.'

The four of them, two holding up a third, and Billy looking as weak as Benson, moved toward the doorway. Where Benson had his helpers pause on the livery's threshold so he could direct a grimace back over his shoulder, challenged:

'One thing you'd better keep in mind, Steele?'

67

'What's that?'

'If you ever come to this town again, stay clear of the Red Dog Saloon.'

Steele nodded. 'Plan to, for a couple of reasons.'

Jacko corrected grimly: 'There are four, mister, and you're lookin' at them.'

The Virginian ignored him, said: 'The bartender doesn't sell coffee. And I don't like the kind of sore losers who play cards at the place.'

'Shit, we ain't sore losers!' Phil countered. 'It's just we don't like bein' took——'

'Forget it, for frig sake!' Jacko snarled.

'Yeah, forget it,' Benson agreed, and they went out.

York announced bitterly: 'Somethin' I ain't gonna forget, stranger! And that's to charge you for me takin' care of them horses and that wagon of yours.'

Steele reached into a hip pocket. 'Me neither. I always pay what I owe.'

'Be five bucks,' York demanded, an avaricious glint in his eyes as he came away from the wall between the stove and the gun rack.

'No it won't,' Steele answered as the mumbling voices of the Red Dog men diminished in the distance.

'What's that you say?' It was anger that shone in the old-timer eyes now.

'Service I had here wouldn't cost me more than a dollar in Providence.'

York scowled. 'Providence? That the one-horse town you come from?'

'I come from Virginia, feller. Valley south of here is where I live now.'

York spat on the floor, started to contend: 'Well, this ain't Providence, so you can——'

Steele cut in: 'This isn't anyplace that's worth more than a buck for what I asked for and got.'

He screwed up a dollar bill in a gloved hand, tossed it toward the liveryman. The scowling York moved with considerable agility for a man of his age to catch the balled up bill. Yelled with heavy menace as Steele drove the wagon out through the wide enough open doors the Red Dog men had neglected to close:

'Mr Whitey Burnett's a friend of mine! He's gonna be madder than ever at you when I tell him about how bad you treated me!'

'That's two strikes against you, York,' Steele called over his shoulder. 'Not just a greedy sonofabitch, you have lousy taste in friends, too!'

The old-timer hurled a string of profanities after the slow-rolling wagon. And at first this abuse was muffled by the sounds of hooves, creaking timbers and turning wheels. Then York placed himself beyond earshot of the subject of his range, slammed the doors closed.

The four gamblers were still in sight, moving disconsolately north on Front, and they directed a series of ugly glances back at Steele. Before he swung the wagon on to Second Street to become lost to view.

The sun would be almost down behind the thick clouds now, he guessed. And maybe the murky light of dusk just made it seem the breeze coming off the lake had a sharper bite to it. But he took his sheepskin coat from out of the back of the wagon, shrugged into it as he drove.

He could see some familiar looking figures on Second, beyond the California Avenue intersection, going toward Pacific. Four women and one man. They carried armsful of purchases or wheeled heavily laden pushcarts.

Only Rufus Grimes was still at the Calendar house when Steele reined his team to a halt behind the auctioneer's buggy. The dapper little man stood in the open doorway of the late druggist's house, silhouetted against the lamplit hallway. He grinned to show he had not really been seriously concerned as he called:

'I was beginning to think you weren't coming back, sir.'

'Had some trouble,' Steele told him, swung down from the wagon, failed on this occasion to sense any hostile watching eyes at the upstairs front window of the Falls house.

'Trouble?' Grimes echoed anxiously.

'Nothing serious.' Steele leaned into the rear of the wagon, dragged from it a folded sheet of burlap, draped it over a front wheel.

'What kind of trouble?' Grimes sounded just mildly interested, like he had irksome problems of his own but felt it right to be politely concerned about those of the other man.

'Some fellers I played cards with at the Red Dog Saloon reckoned I should give them back the money I won off them. I didn't.'

Grimes clapped a hand to a cheek, exclaimed: 'Oh, my Lord! I should have warned you about Benson and those cronies of his I suppose. But I never thought. What with having so much on my mind concerned with the sale, and Mrs Johnson dying, and——'

'It was no big thing,' Steele interrupted evenly, crossed the yard, stepped up on the stoop of the Calendar house. 'Like I said, it was nothing serious.'

Grimes backed into the hallway, said in a manner of making an admission: 'There's a little trouble in connection with a couple of items in the sale, Mr Steele.'

He was close to being obsequious as he picked up the glowing lamp—one of the pair the Virginian had bought— and ushered Steele toward the parlour.

Steele paused on the threshold of the room, asked: 'Items I bought?'

"No!' Grimes blurted. 'No, everything for which you bid successfully is ready and waiting for you to take away. Of course it is.'

'That's fine. You want to help me load up the heavy stuff, feller?'

The auctioneer nodded too vigorously, grinned too broadly, agreed too eagerly: 'Of course, certainly sir. It will be a pleasure. And afterwards, perhaps we may discuss the problem? Come to some arrangement that is mutually beneficial?'

Steele looked quizzically at the man, concealing the fact that he could guess something of what bothered him. But Grimes was too discomfited to hold the questioning gaze. And Steele said eventually with a shrug:

'Maybe.'

Then he allowed himself to be ushered into the parlour by the man who had broken into a sweat before he started to tote anything heavier than the lamp.

'I was sorry to miss out on that,' Steele said, nodded toward the writing bureau.

It and the two bookcases he had bought were all that remained in the room.

Grimes cleared his throat, looked at Steele, quickly away again. Swallowed hard, said thickly: 'That's one of the items I'd like to discuss with you, Mr Steele?'

'One of the problems?'

'Uh...?' He cleared his throat again. 'Yes, that's it. Precisely.'

'Let's load my stuff, talk later about what's bothering you?'

'Certainly, sir.'

To guard against the danger of breaking the glass panels of the bookcase doors they first removed all the volumes. Carried these out to the wagon an armful at a time, then moved the cases. Next the box of carpentry tools was transferred to the wagon, the second kerosene lamp and the watercolour seascapes.

While he was upstairs, Steele saw that the wardrobe that had interested him remained where he had last seen it in the bedroom. The doors were open to show it was empty of clothes now.

Outside, by the wagon, Grimes sweated even more heavily as he hurried to explain: 'Before you say anything, Mr Steele?'

'About your problems, Mr Grimes?'

'The wardrobe.'

'I'm not going to shift anything I didn't buy, feller.'

'No, no! Lars Johannsen, the gentleman who outbid you for the wardrobe? He really only wanted the clothing it contained, sir.'

'That so?'

'Yes, precisely. That is correct. He and the late Mr Calendar were of similar build, you see.'

'That's good.'

71

Grimes pumped his head, mopped at his brow, hurried on: 'Knowing how you had set your sights on having that particular item... And knowing the clothing would be of no use to you... Well, I allowed Mr Johannsen to take the clothes alone. For just two dollars. Returned to him the balance. I'd like you to accept the wardrobe, sir. *Gratis*, if you understand me?'

'For nothing, feller?'

'Precisely.' He licked his lips, pulled a face that seemed to suggest the moisture he tasted was highly salted by sweat.

'You'll help me load it, too?'

'Certainly.'

They went inside the house again, and up the stairs to bring down the wardrobe. Loaded it in the light of the kerosene lamp set down on the stoop of the deceased man's house, augmented by that which spilled out from the downstairs windows of the flanking houses.

'Mr Steele?' Grimes queried as he watched the Virginian make a fast survey of the street after the loading chore was completed.

'Now we'll get to your problem,' Steele offered.

'No, I was going to say: I notice you seem very concerned with our surroundings, sir?'

Steele nodded. 'Yeah, it's just I've been told to get out of Broadwater by sundown.'

'By Benson and his cronies?' Grimes started a wan smile. 'I should not take too much notice of——'

'By one of your lawmen.'

'My Lord, you certainly have gotten yourself into all kinds of trouble since you came to town, Mr Steele?'

'Sometimes that seems to be the story of my life, Mr Grimes,' Steele said with an almost imperceptible sigh as he peered around again at the darkened street splashed with areas of light from house windows. 'I can't see anyone right now who wants to make trouble for me. So, what's your problem, feller?'

He made to slide the folded burlap sheet off the wheel rim. Paused when Grimes said:

'No! Not yet, please?'

The auctioneer worried his lower lip with his teeth, pulled an uglier face than when he licked beads of sweat off both lips earlier. Then he abandoned attempts at evasion, drew in a deep breath, blurted: 'All right, I know you've figured out I'm stuck with the writing bureau in the parlour, right?'

Steele remained silent, waited for Grimes to admit:

'And it's the same with those kitchen items you bid for.'

Then the Virginian nodded, asked: 'How much did you pay the Bonney woman to jack up the prices, feller?'

Grimes said defensively: 'It was just those two lots and I——'

'Those two, and the wardrobe the Swede wanted for the clothes inside, were the only pieces with any kind of value I bid for and didn't get. How much did you waste on the Bonney woman?'

The auctioneer sucked in another deep breath of the chill evening air. He did not sweat out here in the open as he replied nervously: 'I have not said I paid anybody anything, Mr Steele.'

'All right,' the Virginian allowed. 'But you better know I'm not going to pay anything for your mistakes. How much do you want for the two lots you're stuck with?'

'I let you have the wardrobe for nothing, you recall?'

'No, you didn't. I don't want any favours. I pay for what I have from people like you.'

Grimes looked insulted, then he shrugged. 'Very well. Johannsen bid nine dollars. And I gave him back seven. So will you pay me seven for it?'

'Sure.'

Encouraged, Grimes suggested: 'Well, I guess you have to feel the bureau and the kitchen stuff are worth the amounts you bid? Before you withdrew and allowed Clara Bonney to buy?'

'But she didn't.'

'No, she did not, but . . .' He shrugged again, defeated.

'As I recall, I bid fourteen dollars for the bureau, ten for the kitchen stuff?'

'I recollect those same figures, Mr Steele.' Grimes showed the start of a smile.

'I've agreed to give you seven for the wardrobe. For the other two lots, I'll pay twelve dollars, take them off your hands.'

'That's half what you bid at the sale!' Grimes blurted, the embryo smile suddenly gone. 'Most certainly not.'

Steele shifted the burlap sheet, began to unfold it, said: 'It's been a pleasure doing honest business with you, feller.'

Grimes hurried to explain: 'Please understand, my commission is of minimal importance, Mr Steele. I have in mind the unfortunate Mr Ezra Jackson. Whose wife died so tragically just this morning. If you had been able to buy without competition, the paltry sums obtained for the poor, bereaved gentleman would——'

Steele interrupted his chore with the burlap, thrust some bills toward Grimes, cut in on him: 'I'm already mourning somebody I knew. Leaves me short on sympathy for a total stranger. Here's the seven bucks for the wardrobe. Maybe you can raise something on the other stuff from the local pawnbroker?'

Crestfallen, Grimes accepted the money with his right hand. Transferred it to the left. Then grunted as he reached a snap decision, pushed out the right again, said grudgingly: 'Very well, pay me the other twelve: take the damn bureau and kitchen junk!'

Steele set down the burlap, shook his head. 'No feller. First you give me a hand to load the extra stuff. Then I'll pay you. In case you're that cheating kind who takes the money and runs.'

'I resent that, sir! And I——'

'I need to hurry if I'm to stay out of trouble with the local law, feller.'

'Oh, very well!' Grimes snarled with a glare, then spun around and moved across the yard toward the front door of the Calendar house.

As Steele followed him, a darkened window in the side of the Falls house cracked open and a familiar voice taunted in a rasping whisper:

'So you finally did get to screw somebody today, mister?'

'Dolly, you say somethin'?' a man's voice called from an upstairs room and the window banged closed.

The girl answered her father loudly enough for what she said to reach the ears of Steele and Grimes despite the closed window: 'Yeah, Pa—I just seen a rat in next door's front yard!'

The bureau was heavy and had it not been for the chill lake breeze probably both men would have sweated getting it out of the house, on to the rear of the wagon. Transferring the final sale lot was simply irksomely time consuming: entailed several back and forth trips, much as with the books earlier. Steele left the dilapidated storage cabinet in the otherwise empty house.

When they were through, Grimes locked the front door and waited patiently for Steele to finish tying down the burlap sheet over his purchases. Then, after the Virginian had given him the twelve dollars and climbed up on the wagon seat, the auctioneer said:

'You drive a hard bargain, Steele.' Now their business was concluded, it was pointedly apparent he had dropped any form of courtesy title. But he spoke without rancour.

'Far as I'm concerned, I'm driving a wagonload of bargains,' Steele replied with a quiet smile. 'Since the fellers from the Red Dog Saloon sprang for them for me.'

'That, I must allow, is something that pleases me greatly, Steele,' Grimes answered, genuinely happy at the news. 'That Buddy Benson and his cronies have gypped enough people in their time. I guess they should have known better than to try to swindle a man like you?'

He saw Steele eyed him with irony, showed a sardonic smile of his own as he added; 'But then I didn't, did I?'

'Turns out other people's losses are my gains. I'm not complaining.'

'I certainly learned an expensive lesson. But as an auctioneer, perhaps I should say, thanks a lot?' His smile had become amiable.

Steele gestured with an arm to encompass the back of his laden wagon. Said: 'I'm thankful for all these lots, feller.'

Grimes' face was spread with a broad grin as he countered: 'Again, as an auctioneer, I bid you good evening.'

'Yeah.' Steele took up the reins, prepared to swing the team out around the buggy parked directly ahead of his rig. Paused to listen to Grimes' promise:

'Something you can be rest assured of, Mr Steele. If you ever attend another of my sales, I'll make no attempt to raise the prices by unfair means.'

'And you can rest assured, Mr Grimes,' Steele replied flatly, 'that if you try it, I'll knock you down. And then hammer you into the ground.'

7

Steele drove slowly along the night-shrouded California Avenue: out past the town limits marker and on to the open trail toward home. Tense behind apparent nonchalance to pick up signs he was under surveillance by the glowering eyes of men who meant him nothing good.

But his mysterious sixth sense for lurking danger failed to trigger any warning within his receptive mind. Then he became even more alert behind the façade as he drove the team at the same unhurried pace up the open lower slope of the hillside beyond the south side of Broadwater. Devoted as much time to looking back toward the town as peering at the point where the trail entered the timber.

Behind him, now that moonless night had come to the Sierra Nevada foothills, Broadwater's reputation as the only bright-lights town for hundreds of miles around was vividly re-established. For from this elevated position on the rise, not only Front Street blazed with lights mirrored on the breeze rippled surface of Providence Lake. Less garish, but cheerfully bright nonetheless, were the lights of the two parallel residential avenues and the connecting side streets.

Out on this open lower half of the gentle slope, the evening breeze tugged at Steele's hat, chilled his stubbled face beneath. And he welcomed the warmth of the sheepskin coat buttoned tightly around him. Then, once he was confident he was not being watched by aggressively inclined men from the town or out of the timber, he began to relish a different brand of warmth.

That the warmth of contentment as he reflected on what he

had achieved from his afternoon stay in Broadwater.

He could have done without the trouble, that was for sure. Especially that which got him on the wrong side of Gavin Fenton's new deputy. He was bothered less by the run-in with Burnett who obviously had strong connections with the plushest saloon in town. And he had meant what he told Benson and his buddies about having no hankering to return to the Red Dog Saloon. There were plenty more games in town, providing Dexter's edict applied only to today.

But if the worst came to the worst . . . Like he often said, a man had to take the rough with the smooth. And maybe it could turn out for the best if he remained unwelcome anywhere in Broadwater. For then he would not be prey to the temptations of the bright lights town.

As he drove the wagon into the darkness of the timber under the roof-like arch of overhanging foliage, this line of thought did little to detract from the sense of satisfaction drawn from the achievements of the day. Then the feeling of well-being heightened as he ceased to reflect upon the immediate past: visualised what lay in his future at Trail's End. Where, despite having to contend with more than a fair share of obstacles placed in his path, the many mistakes he had made, and having had his good intentions misinterpreted so often, he was managing to make a go of the spread.

And, it struck him suddenly, it was another measure of success that he was driving this wagon toward Trail's End, loaded with more of what a man needed to secure the roots he was determined to put down in a home of his own. Now he had set aside earlier ambitions to live the high life: and had given up the freedom of the open trail.

Freedom!

The word reverberated through his mind: then became firmly fixed there. In such a way he found himself bound to question if he had maybe surrendered one of life's most precious possessions in exchange for the settled existence at Trail's End. And could it be the many trials and tribulations he had needed to overcome—and others he surely still faced—in putting down those roots, were created by the cruel fates he at one time considered ruled his life? Fates which were now only mischievous in the way they attempted to convince him such a burdensome life was not worth the price he had paid?

No, the hell with that! He was doing fine, damnit. And if he ever had any regrets, got attacked by doubts, they were easy to deal with: he had only to count his blessings.

He had not ceased to be aware of his surroundings, their potential for hidden danger, after the wagon rolled off the exposed hillside into the timber: and he allowed his mind to wander at will. For he knew it would be easier for vengeance-bent men to spring an ambush in the deep cover of the trees. So he waited and listened as carefully as before, ready to counter such an attack: make use of the same cover also available to him in the wooded darkness.

The horses and wagon moving unhurriedly along the summer-hardened surface of the trail made the only discernible sounds. Ahead of the plodding team, the pale strip of the trail against the flanking dark of the trees was all that could be seen.

But then his sense of smell signalled something was maybe not as it should be. And he saw from the reactions of the horses as they pricked their ears, tossed their heads, softly whinnied their uneasiness through flared nostrils, that they had also caught a trace of smoke in the air. An ugly, acrid taint that became gradually stronger in the fresh, chill night after the hot day had released so many, more pleasant, fragrances of grass, brush, trees and the nearby river.

It was not the new smoke smell of present burning. So he knew when he got to its source he would not find a warming fire. Or, even better since it was so long ago he ate the greasy food at the restaurant of the garrulous couple, a warming fire under a pot that gave off steam aromatic with the appetising fragrance of fresh-brewed coffee, a skillet of frying meat.

Instead, it was the dry, stale stink of a long dead fire. Which reached far enough through the timber to be much bigger than one lit to cook supper at a night camp beside a stretch of

79

trail Steele abruptly realised he recognised.

He was beside a massive escarpment that lay between the age-old course of the river and the relatively new, man-made trail. Would soon emerge at the southern end of the rocky bluff, beyond which the trail followed a curved line alongside the east bank of the river.

Not so many months ago, when the river was in noisy full flood with mountain melt water spilling over the rapids at the mouth of a nearby gorge, a youngster had been tragically, wastefully killed here. Now, Steele saw, not far from where the Providence vigilantes had set up their ambush and made a prisoner of the scared kid, earlier today another trap had been laid and sprung. And as he recognised what had happened, who it had happened to, he was gripped by an tense feeling of guilt which was somehow made more painful by the way the clouds now parted, allowed moonlight to shaft brightly down on the riverside scene of destruction.

Today's ambushers had forced the Garcia wagon to a halt further around the curve of the river and trail in the direction of Providence: three telegraph poles along from the one on which the innocent kid had been accidentally hanged.

He knew at first glance it was the Garcia wagon that had been hit. Stretched seconds before he recognised the slight figures as the three Mexicans moved out of the moon shadowed trees: the father with a daughter at either side of him. Hugging them around their shoulders to press the small girls against his legs. They halted beside the sprawl of charred timber, blackened ironwork and grey ashes that comprised the remains of their wagon. Close by were the humped carcases of the burros that had been slaughtered in the traces where they were halted.

As Steele reined in his team he glimpsed some familiar shapes close to where Garcia and the girls stood, their previously almost white travel-stained clothes streaked and smudged with soot from the fire: the frame and grinding stones that fitted it. In the poor light the equipment did not look to be badly fire scarred and Steele guessed the Mexican himself had dragged the tools of his trade clear of the flames.

It was unlikely the people responsible for the wanton destruction of the wagon, the killing of the animals, would have done so...

Then Steele tried to force his mind to adopt a more constructive line of thought. But he could think only of his guilt.

'*La culpa es suya!*' the taller, older girl snarled at him as his wagon came to rest, the two horses made slight sounds of equine distress at being so close to the dead animals.

'*Collarse!*' Garcia snapped. Was obviously on the verge of a greater fury than he showed as he spoke what sounded like rebuke at Conchita.

Then there was a fast exchange between father and elder daughter. While Maria seemed gripped by deep shock, simply stared into the middle distance, the total lack of expression on her pretty face giving no clue to what she saw there: in reality or imagination.

The talk was low toned. Steele thought idly he may have caught some of it, were it spoken in his own language. Then Conchita became sullenly submissive, resentfully persuaded to her father's point of view. And Esteban Garcia hugged both his daughters more closely to him.

Steele, still seated on the wagon, finally said: 'They really made you pay high for what I did to Whitey Burnett, feller.'

Garcia seemed to think about this for several moments. Then he shook his head dismissively, ignored the Virginian's opening. Proclaimed; 'We are so happy to see you, *señor*. At first, Conchita was angry. She is now sorry for what she said to you.'

Steele shrugged, then said as he climbed to the ground: 'Longest I was ever in Mexico I was drunk for weeks on end.' He went to stand between his two horses, calmed the final traces of nervousness out of them by stroking their noses. 'So I was in no fit state to learn much of the language.'

'I said all this was your fault,' Conchita explained without a trace of regret in her voice or her face—less pretty than that of her sister—which tonight looked even older than usual. 'I am sorry I said so.'

Since she was so young, Steele chose not to draw the possible inference she was sorry only that she had voiced the feeling: that she nonetheless still felt it. He elected, also, to ignore the temptation to confide that he thought the kid was partially right. He was partly to blame.

Garcia displayed a smile that showed he had lost a lower front tooth. And as he moved his head Steele saw also the Mexican had a swollen right eye and a blood-crusted gash on his left cheek. He explained eagerly: 'I tell my daughters it is best for us to wait here, *amigo*. That you *Señor* Steele will return home after you have completed your *negocio* ... your business in the town of Broadwater. They do not agree this is best.' He looked down at each of the girls, hugged them again. 'Now they see their *papa* is right, uh?'

'It seems they don't particularly like what they see,' Steele said grimly, then shrugged, added: 'But after what happened here, I guess it's natural they're going to have a grudge against the world.'

'*Si, señor*!' Garcia said quickly, increasingly eager to agree with Steele. '*Le gente menudo* do not understand so well, uh? They have seen so little about the *gringos–como—* the Americans to make them trust anybody who is not Mexican. They see all Americans like the kind of *malicioso hombres* who have done this to us.'

He grimaced, waved a hand over the blackened wreckage of the burned wagon, the dead burros.

'The bunch from the Blue Moon Saloon?' Steele asked.

The Mexican sighed deeply, replied absently: 'I expect so, *señor*.'

'You mean you don't know? Didn't you recognise any of them? It was still light when you——'

Garcia again came close to losing the tenuous grip on his temper. After taking a few moments to bring himself under firm control, he shook his head, cut in: 'No, *señor*. It was so *rapido*. And dark as we come to this place. A *lazo* is thrown over me. I do not know of this when it happens. I know then there is much noise. Much shouting. My daughters scream, jump from the wagon as I am pulled from it. Run away...'

He started to get deeply angry despite himself: to run words together, increasingly mixed in phrases from his own language. Was in danger of becoming unintelligible.

Steele held up both hands, which made the elder sister flinch, left Maria unmoved: still held fast in a state of shock.

'Easy,' the Virginian said. 'Look, why don't you tell me the rest of it while we head down the trail?'

It took a stretched second for Garcia to register what Steele had said to him. Then he nodded, eager again. Apparently ignored what Conchita rasped at him in their own language. Until he again snapped:

'*Collarse*!'

Steele now guessed this meant for her to shut up, for this is what she did, with bad grace. Then Garcia's punished face spread with another smile as he agreed:

'*Si, Señor* Steele. That will be best. You are most kind to——'

'Let's get your stuff on the wagon?'

Garcia nodded, let go of his daughters. And as this contact was lost, Maria began to howl. Without being asked, Conchita began to comfort her sister while their father brought the frame and circular stones to the side of the wagon. Steele opened up a section of the burlap cover and the two men loaded the equipment aboard. Space was left so that Garcia could lift up his daughters in turn and place them in the back of the wagon.

While Steele watched this he had the thought that if he attempted to help, the calming Maria was likely to break out into raucous bawling again while Conchita might try to hit, kick, scratch or bite him.

He climbed up on the wagon seat and after Garcia had gone to retrieve his sombrero, settled himself on the passenger side of the seat, Steele knocked off the brakes, flicked the reins, steered the rig through a curve off the trail between the trees and the wreckage and dead burros. Then, when Maria had given a final sob and the mixed fragrances of moving water and night time timber had masked the stink of old burning, Steele said:

'I thought you'd left town this afternoon, way before sundown? Shouldn't have taken you more than thirty minutes to get to where they hit you.'

Garcia defended: 'I never said, *señor*, that I would leave right after the trouble at the hotel.'

Steele allowed to himself this was true.

In the rear of the wagon, Maria whispered to Conchita and even though he did not understand their language, the Virginian was able to differentiate between the voices of the two young round-faced, brown-eyed, black-haired girls.

'*Con permiso, amigo*,' Garcia said: turned to rattle out another burst of rapid-fire Mexican-Spanish. The tone of his voice indicated he asked a demanding question of his daughters.

They both attempted to speak at once but as usual the older girl won the contest. As she replied sullenly to her father Steele sensed her unblinking eyes focused in a resentful glare on his back.

'*Bueno*,' Garcia announced, turned to face front. Said to Steele: '*Señor*, my daughters now say they know something of these men who attacked us. They did not tell this to me before because they worried I would return to Broadwater: to seek my own revenge. So they *pretender* run away, *paranza* ... They tell me they hid from these *hombres* in *de bosque*. They wait in the trees until the *pistoleros* have gone. They see nothing of what took place.'

He shook his head wearily, fingered the congealed blood on the cut in his cheek. 'This is what they tell me at first. I am now told none of it was true. Conchita now she says the leader of the *hombres* who attack us, it was the one at the hotel with the hair the same white colour as yours, *señor*.'

Steele said: 'It figures. But there was a chance you stirred up some more people: the way you didn't leave right after the trouble with Whitey Burnett.'

Garcia shook his head vigorously, vehemently assured: 'No! No more trouble in the town, *señor*. I ask at many other places about my Carmelita. I learn nothing of her, but nobody is so mean to us as the people at the big hotel. Some they are not so kind, but they make no trouble for us. Others, they are as you, *amigo*. They try to be helpful to us, but unlike you, they cannot be. They have not heard of Carmelita, the mother of these *lastimoso* ... these poor children of ours.'

Esteban Garcia seemed to want to continue, but was unable to do so. He started to rub at his lower belly, then the centre of his chest. Kept his bruised and cut face averted, and Steele thought the Mexican was in considerable pain, did not want anyone to know about it. And the Virginian recalled then how Garcia had seemed so rigidly stiff-jointed as he carried his blade sharpening equipment to the wagon, hefted up his daughter, finally climbed gratefully aboard himself. Realised now this had not been simply an attempt at dignity in adversity. Rather, pride in pain.

There was, though, something else—less obvious— that was wrong about the whole thing. Steele was certain of this, but he kept coming back to the same starting point for the suspicion that nagged him: it was the sense of his own guilt for being the cause of this latest trouble that made him look so deeply for something wrong with this Mexican family which had fallen so heavily on hard times.

Now he once more sensed the eyes of Conchita boring into his back and in the moonlit peace of the timbered river valley disturbed only by the sounds of the horses and wagon, he felt drawn to look over his shoulder at the two huddled-together children. Saw the earnest faces of both girls upturned so their unblinking eyes met his gaze.

He shook his head and looked away, faced front again to concentrate on driving the rig through the dappled moonlight and shade along the winding trail that had now swung away from the river.

Moments later, the older sister said: '*Señor* Steele? When I said to you it was your fault, I did not really mean you are to blame for it all.'

'Conchita, you must not——' her father started to interrupt.

'Let her have her say,' Steele broke in. Did not look back at the girl when he invited: 'I'm listening, young lady.'

She rasped out some fast Mexican-Spanish and Steele reminded:

'I said I don't know your language.'

Garcia explained anxiously: 'Conchita speaks to me, *amigo*. She says she has not told this to me yet. She tells me again the reason why she has lied is because she feared what I would do. I tell you something, *Señor* Steele. I will listen as anxiously as you to what Conchita is to say.'

He looked and sounded on the brink of rage again. Then he showed an expression on his battered features that was no more than paternally stern as he glanced back at his eldest daughter, nodded for her to speak. And she began at once, accompanied every now and then by a sound of agreement from her sister.

'There were five of them, *Señor* Steele. We do not see this at first. We do not see that the man you knocked down outside the big hotel is with them: the leader. When the *lazo*, the rope, was thrown over my *papa*, he fell very hard to the ground. And they jumped on him. They hit him with their fists, kicked him. They laughed and shouted the bad words. We think my *papa* is dead. Then Maria and me, we are lifted off our wagon. This is just as the burros are killed. Shot: bang, bang.'

Garcia interjected tautly: 'Before, I was told they ran to hide in the trees.'

'It is the truth which Conchita tells to you now, *papa*,' Maria assured in grave tones.

Conchita hurried to take up the telling of the story. 'The men take the *keroseno* off their horses, throw it upon the wagon. Maria and me, we try to wake up my *papa* who I know now is not dead. The matches are lit and the fire starts. Maria, she is struck dumb. She thinks still that *papa* is dead.'

'This I truly think, *señor*,' Maria confirmed in the same earnest tone as before.

'I!' Conchita said emphatically and a little irritably to recapture the centre of attention, 'pretend I do not understand what they say to me. Until they say they will truly kill our *papa*, they will throw him into the fire of the wagon, unless I understand.'

'It is true,' Maria assured.

'Now I tell only the truth!' Conchita snapped. 'I tell them I understand and it is then they say it is your fault, what has happened, *Señor* Steele. They say my *papa's amigo* who hurt the man with white hair is to blame. They say I am to tell this to *papa* so he can tell you. But I tell my *papa* none of it until now. Because I am afraid he will get very angry. Try to find you. Or try to——'

'*Bastante!*' Garcia growled.

Conchita translated evenly: '*Papa* says it is enough, *Señor* Steele. Which is true. There is no more to tell. Except——' Her tone became rebuking: 'that the *gringos* do no more than speak bad to Maria and me. They do not hurt us. Sometimes, my *papa* he has——'

Garcia had started to rub the aching areas of his body again. Then he vented a grunt of pain caused when he turned quickly, to peer at his daughters. He began to say something in his native tongue, but paused and translated: 'I tell them, *señor*, it is sometimes necessary for a father to correct his children with firmness. It is sometimes worse for children who have no mother who perhaps knows better how to——'

'*Si papa*, I know,' Maria said quickly.

'Me, too,' Conchita added contritely. 'I am sorry to say what I did.'

The way the girl phrased the apology once again suggested an implication she did not say precisely what was in her mind.

Steele said: 'It all right if I ask a couple of questions?'

'*Como no,*' Garcia said eagerly.

Conchita said: 'My *papa* says of course you may, *señor*.'

'When Burnett—that's the white haired feller—and the rest of them were through, which way did they go?'

Conchita replied in a knowing tone of voice: 'Toward the town of Broadwater, *señor*. They rode their horses fast. There was much laughter as they left.'

'Did any of them mention me by name?'

Again he got the impression it was a question Conchita had expected when she replied:

'No, *señor*. I did not hear your name spoken by them.'

87

'I'm grateful.'

'You are most welcome, *señor*.'

Garcia said morosely: 'We are so sorry we cause you so much trouble.'

Steele acknowledged this latest apology with a non-committal grunt. His mind that had earlier been nagged by guilt about the Mexican family was now occupied with another cause for concern. And he ignored the discomfited father and older-than-her-years daughter.

But, like he had read the mind of the Virginian, Esteban Garcia said: 'I think you are anxious that they know who you are, *señor*? But you know if they rode back to Broadwater, they will not be waiting in hiding between here and where you live, is that not so?'

Steele answered absently: 'It's one assumption, feller.'

Once more they drove without talk for some time. While Steele convinced himself that Conchita would not have lied about the direction in which Burnett and the others rode off. And mulled over the possibility that they could have turned around, made a wide swing to head south down the valley. But it made no sense. They would not take the time and trouble to do that. If they knew he was still in Broadwater, there was plenty of dark trail between town and the bend in the river where they could have waited for him.

But if they knew his name, found out where he lived . . .?

Steele made a throaty sound of disgust with himself for indulging in the futile pursuit of looking for trouble where it most probably did not exist.

As he became aware again of the predicament which currently trapped him, he sensed the expanding atmosphere of discomfiture aboard the slow rolling wagon: guessed there were questions his passengers itched to ask him. But neither the father nor his eldest daughter found it easy to put them. And he certainly felt no obligation to smooth the path for the man or the child to speak what was on their minds.

Then, eventually, Esteban Garcia stopped dry-washing his hands, cleared his throat and asked out of the blue: 'You live outside the town of Providence, *señor*?'

'You know it.'

'*Si*, you say as much last night. When I was *estupido* enough to aim my pistol at you.'

'Yeah,' Steele murmured. 'Hey, what happened to that old Colt revolver, feller?'

He sighed. 'It was lost in the fire. After I recovered from what the *bast*—the bad *hombres*—did to me, I was able only to get my tools out of the flames. But I go from the point. You live some way off from the town of Providence, do you not?'

'On a spread called Trail's End.'

'*Si*, where you raise the fine horses. I have heard this.'

'People talk.'

Conchita made a throat clearing sound of disapproval.

Her father hastened to repair any misunderstanding. 'When I was working to sharpen blades in Providence, *señor*, I speak of the funeral I have seen. There is some talk of the people who were there. The people who *lamentar*...mourn. You know how it is?'

'Yeah, I've been in that town often enough to know how it is,' Steele muttered, irritated at himself for the puerile reason he did not make it easy for Garcia to ask the question he guessed was on the mind of the Mexican.

'It is *solitario*... you understand?'

'Isolated, *papa*,' Conchita prompted.

'*Si, gracias*. Isolated at the Trail's End *hacienda*. And you live there alone?'

Steele replied flatly: 'I wouldn't call it a *hacienda*, feller. That brings to my mind a big place. But right, it's way out in the country. And I live there alone, which is how I like it.'

Garcia signalled he was getting close to the point. Gave an abrupt cough that did little to smooth the roughness of embarrassment out of his voice when he said: 'My two daughters and me are not liked by many people in Providence, *señor*. You know this. Because we are Mexicans. You know, too, we are *desprovisto* and far from our home. Tonight, if you have places for Conchita and Maria to sleep at your *haci*... at your place, I will be most pleased to stand guard. Watch for the unwelcome visitors?'

89

Steele needed consciously to take a firmer control on the mounting exasperation he felt as much with himself as the Garcia family and the men from the Blue Moon Saloon. He came within a part of a second of growling sourly that all visitors at Trail's End were unwelcome.

Then it was as if Maria Garcia mysteriously read what had come unbidden into his mind. And as the younger of the two girls spoke Steele realised why he always knew which one was talking: Maria had an engaging slight lisp.

'I promise I will not cry any more, *señor*. Nor make any noise, except to speak when I am spoken to. I do dishes real well. Also I will brush the dirt from the floor if I am asked. Feed your animals and also——'

Conchita interrupted her sister in their native language, her sharp tone conveying she was ticking off Maria.

Garcia translated: 'My older daughter reminds her sister we are not poor and humble *mendigos* . . . beggers, uh? Maria must not try so hard to win——'

'Yeah, I've got the message,' Steele said, sighed.

'So *señor*?'

Steele did not take his eyes off the trail ahead, but knew the man seated beside him and the two children riding in the back of the heavily laden wagon peered at him with avid expectation, willing him to respond positively to what they wanted.

'Yeah,' he said. 'Okay. I guess I owe you a night's bed and board, at least.'

The girls made small sounds as they contained their excitement.

Garcia asked anxiously: 'Owe us, *señor*? I do not understand this. I am grateful for your offer to help, but——'

Steele broke in: 'If I hadn't taken a hand in your trouble at the Blue Moon, it would have finished there and then for you. You'd have been spared what happened back up the trail.'

'No, *señor*!' Garcia countered with a sudden impassioned emphasis that triggered a jolt of pain which forced him to clutch at his narrow chest with both hands. 'I cannot agree with this you say! If you did not help in the trouble at the hotel, I would have lost a daughter, not just an old wagon and two broken down burros. I know which of this is the more precious to me, *señor*.'

Steele looked over his shoulder. Found both girls peering fixedly back with matching doe-eyed gazes. He pulled a face, shook his head, growled: 'Yeah.'

Conchita said evenly: 'I think, *Señor* Steele, you do not like children so much?'

The Virginian answered sardonically: 'I can't say if I do or not, young lady. I always find I bite off more than I can chew with kids. So I haven't really ever gotten to taste one yet.'

8

Whatever else was not quite right about the Mexican family
and the way Steele had come to be landed with them at Trail's
End, it was not the injuries suffered by the slightly-built, lean-
featured, eager-to-please Esteban Garcia.

The Virginian had already seen the gap from the missing
tooth, the bruises and cuts on his face. And saw that the man
was hurt worse than this after he rolled the rig to a halt on the
yard formed by the house, the corral, the barn and the two
crop fields at Trail's End. Realised by the way the Mexican
got gingerly down from the wagon, was unable to contain a
low groan, clutched at his side and made a point of staring
fixedly out into the night so his expression could not be seen,
it was likely he could also have a cracked, maybe a broken rib.

In which event, Steele knew, the ride aboard the jolting
wagon must have been far more painful for Garcia than he
had shown.

Inside the shack which still had just the one habitable
room, Garcia lowered himself gratefully on to a hard seated,
straight backed chair at the pine table in the kitchen area.
Made only a token protest as Steele helped him to take off his
shirt and undershirt while Conchita and Maria busied
themselves with lighting the lamps and the kindling in the
stove. When his clothing was removed it was seen the man
had areas of purple and yellow bruising across his chest and
lower back, two blackened patches on the left side of his belly
and some congealed blood on the right side where a fist or
boot had landed hard enough to split the skin.

So, whatever else, Esteban Garcia had certainly taken one

hell of a beating out there on the dark trail south of Broadwater before they burned his wagon and killed his animals.

Once they had seen just how badly their father was hurt, both little girls now seemed immediately to be far older than their tender years. Began to treat him like he was the youngest member of their family: adopted matriarchal attitudes toward their father and Adam Steele that had both men do their bidding without question.

At first Garcia needed constantly to translate much that was said, the small girls too worried about their father's injuries to think about expressing themselves in a foreign language. And he apologised often for the way Conchita and Maria made so many imperious demands upon their host.

But Steele soon came to welcome the way things were turning out. For he was able to leave the injured man in the young but obviously capable hands of the girls. Confident they would do no harm to their father or to his home. So he could go outside, attend to the wagon and team: managed with some difficulty but without help to unload his purchases. Stowed the furniture and other items in a stall at the stable end of the barn, covered with a burlap sheet. Garcia's stuff he left on the wagon.

When he left the barn he saw that smoke was curling from the chimney of the house, the light from the windows flanking the front door was dimmer than earlier. On the threshold he was greeted by the delicious aroma of meat cooking on the stove and the subdued sounds of a man breathing easily in a much-needed sleep.

The Mexican was in Steele's bed, just his head visible on the pillow. But the Virginian's initial impulse to anger at the presumption of the Garcia family was immediately quelled. This when he saw the table had been set. And how the two small girls beside the stove looked at him, presenting another tableau of doe-eyed innocence.

The food smelled good and it was easy to accept without protest their dictate that he should wash up before supper. They had already taken care of themselves in this respect.

And despite his thick growth of stubble, it could be seen the girls had made sure their father cleaned off the trail dust and fire soot before they bedded him down.

While Steele went along with the latest wishes of the Garcia children he recalled with a sharp pang of grief the way Arlene Forrester had been when she summoned him and—damnit, more grief—Billy Baxter to come to breakfast or the midday meal on her mornings to work at Trail's End. Females of any age, nation or colour certainly did seem to enjoy bossing a man about, he reflected with a fleeting smile within the cover of the towel he used to dry off his face.

The three ate together at the pine table and it could have been an uncomfortable meal shared by a bachelor—Steele never acknowledged his marriage to Lucy Girard down in Texas—and the two children who never uttered a word after Conchita completed a short, fast-spoken grace.

But he felt no kind of awkwardness as he reflected upon his purchases at the sale in Broadwater. Planned where the pieces of furniture would go in the two rooms he intended to make from this one, and in the bedroom extension. Which was as yet just a shell of three additional walls and a half roof set at right angles to the present bedroom and parlour area. On the other side of the wall near the bed which was marked with the outline for the connecting doorway.

Occasionally, when Esteban Garcia moved in his sleep, punctuated his steady breathing with a grunt of discomfort, Steele was jerked out of his pleasant contemplation of domestic affairs: reminded of his unexpected guests. But Garcia always sank back into restful sleep. And the anxious frowns on the immature faces of the two small girls would be replaced by smiles of relief.

Seeing this, the Virginian discovered his nagging suspicion about the Garcia family all but gone. Sometimes even felt something close to a stir of affection toward the children. Such a situation did not last for long, though. And soon he would have to remind himself that the Mexican family would be gone in the morning: only thus could he ease renewed doubts from his mind.

94

After the meal of bacon, eggs, beans and toasted stale bread, Conchita fussed over Steele. Insisted he take his ease in the winged chair by the open-fronted bookcase where he invariably sat to read for awhile at the end of a hard day working the spread. She would bring him a cup of coffee there, she promised. But whether she did or not, Steele never knew. For after he willingly settled into the chair, decided he was too tired even to reach for one of the books in the nearby less-than-elegant bookcase that would soon be replaced by one of the glass-fronted versions bought at the sale, he abruptly sank into a deep sleep. Just a moment, it seemed, after his leaden eyelids came together and he sensed a total inability to move a single muscle.

It was the strange kind of heavy sleep that seems to last for just a short time. In which dreams fill the sub-conscious mind only in the final seconds before sudden waking. Dreams that are so vivid they seem more real than reality: summoned by emotions that are stronger than a man is able to experience in the actual situation he can trace as the cause of the dreams.

At first, Steele was certain he had drifted into a light sleep that lasted just a few minutes at the most. So when he snapped open his eyes he sniffed eagerly to catch the expected aroma of the cup of coffee the Mexican girl had promised to bring him.

But he realised at once that the light against which he blinked was far too bright to be from the kerosene lamps: which Maria Garcia had said she was going to dim even more as soon as she and her sister finished clearing the table and doing the dishes.

Not only was the light wrong, either. There was no aroma of fresh brewed coffee in the house. Or a smell of cooking.

Damnit, a new day had dawned!

He straightened up from being slumped low in the winged chair, legs splayed in front. Peered through the window beside him. Out across the yard, the corral on the other side, and beyond this the south western section of the three and a half thousand rolling acres of fine grazing land that comprised the Trail's End property.

Because he looked westward, the bright morning sun did not stream its light directly into the room at him. He could tell by the length of the shadows cast by the house, the corral fence and the child who stood in the centre of the yard that it was still early. He guessed no later than an hour or so since the first rays of the sun shafted down over the Sierra Nevadas ridges far off in back of the house. Maybe as long as six or seven hours since he fell so suddenly to sleep. Maybe, too, he dreamed throughout this entire period about how he could not let the situation stay as it was ...

Within the space of a few more fleeting seconds he had recalled memories of last night's events beyond the good food he ate and anticipation of the coffee that never came. Commanded clear memories triggered by his dreams and the reality of seeing Conchita Garcia who stood on the centre of the yard. Like a carved statue for a moment, until the slightly built little girl turned in a slow circle, to sweep an intent, searching gaze toward every point of the compass.

When she looked at the house the low sun shone full in her eyes, made her squint. She gave no sign she could see in through the window to where Steele now got up from the chair, grimacing as muscles stiffened from resting in one position so long protested the movement.

He double-checked the interior of the house. Saw first his recollection of Esteban Garcia sleeping in his bed was sound. Next that the younger Garcia girl was not in the house; but wherever she was, the two sisters had cleaned up every trace of whatever mess they made in tending to their father's injuries and cooking supper. The place was as clean and neat as it had ever been in the old days when Arlene Forrester had completed the household chores.

'You do not recall what took place yesterday, *señor*?'

Steele was momentarily startled by the query from the Mexican, who rolled his head to the side of the pillow, peered toward the Virginian with an expresssion of concern on his features which looked even more badly beaten now that bright daylight shone on every lean angle of his unshaven face.

'What's that, feller?'

'You seem puzzled, *mi amigo*.' Garcia showed an expression that might have been a scowl but for the warm brightness of a smile he was able to generate in his dark eyes. 'Like you do not remember too well what happened? Or maybe you remember this, but you regret doing as you did to help us?'

Steele shook his head, crooked a forefinger, tapped his temple, replied: 'It's all real clear in here now.' He let the hand trail down his cheek, rasping over his own twenty-four hours growth of bristles. 'How are you doing, Garcia?'

'I have felt better, *señor*.' He tried to sit up in the bed, but raised his back only a few inches before he grimaced and collapsed. Forced the grimace into a pained grin, admitted: 'Much better, I think. You *amigo*?'

'Yeah, I've felt better, too.'

Concern flooded across the battered face in the wake of the quickly gone grin. 'Because I and the *muchachas* are here in your house? Because we forced our presence upon you? They told me in the night while you slept so deeply, *señor*, how they took it upon themselves to make free with your food and——'

'Your kids did fine,' Steele told him. 'I'd like them to keep on doing fine, with a little help from you, maybe? If you can manage it?'

'Anything, *señor*!' He started to beam, but was at once uneasy again, when he saw Steele did not alter his look of grim intent. Hurried on: 'If it is within my power to do so, of course? You know I am a man of little means. And also, it seems, one whose word is not to be trusted. But I did truly mean to stand the guard in the night. I could not remain awake and——'

'I know how that can be, feller,' Steele cut in. 'But it seems like your daughters took care of that. For both of us.'

'*Si*. Conchita and Maria have taken the turns. One resting in the barn while the other watches for *intrusos*. They tell me they would have awakened us if anyone approached.'

'Like you and your daughters to keep an eye on the place, take care of the stock, for another day?'

'*Señor*, why do you ask this?'

'Because I won't be here to do it for myself.'

'You are leaving?'

'I need to go back to Broadwater.'

'But *señor*! That is a very dangerous town for you. Even if the Burnett *hombre* and his *amigos* do not make trouble for you, there is the matter of the deputy sheriff who tells you to——'

'They're the reasons I need to go back,' Steele broke in. He went to the kitchen end of the room, saw the girls had kept the fire alight, with a pot of gently steaming water on top of the hot stove.

Garcia watched the Virginian stir a greater heat from the fire, put a pot of coffee on to boil and then start to wash up and shave. Said at length:

'I do not understand so much about you, *señor*. But I think you are a man who will stop at nothing to do what he wants to do.'

'I reckon that's right, feller. But it took me a night of sleeping on it to remind myself of that.'

'*Señor*?'

'It sticks in my craw to know I can't go some place on account of somebody saying that I can't,' Steele answered.

And the Mexican had no way of knowing the vehemence in Adam Steele's tone was caused as much by thoughts of the state of Virginia as the town of Broadwater.

'*Señor*, if you will wait for a little while, until I am in not so much pain, we can go together? And maybe the chances of——'

'You have your own problems,' Steele said.

'*Si*, but . . .' Garcia started to rise in the bed. Got his back up a little higher, but was forced to flop down again. Vented a loud groan which carried out into the quiet morning.

Steele wiped off the surplus lather from the shave, glanced through the window at the kitchen end of the house in time to see both the Garcia girls freeze. Maria standing where Conchita had been on watch earlier, while the elder sister had been heading in the direction of the barn. Then, as their surprise at the unexpected sound of pain was replaced by deep concern, they both lunged toward the house door.

Garcia was flat on his back, still grimacing, but silent now. And Steele was starting to put on his gloves when the door burst open and Conchita demanded anxiously:

'*Que sucede, papa?*'

Maria blurted: '*Si, que hay?*'

As the girls looked from their father toward Steele, the man in the bed rasped through gritted teeth:

'*No es para quejarse, muchachas.*' Then, as last night, he hurried to explain for Steele: 'The girls wish to know what is the matter. I tell them I have nothing to complain about. Not like you, uh, *mi amigo?*'

'Complaining has never gotten me anywhere, feller,' Steele said.

Maria went to the bed and Conchita headed for the stove, insisted earnestly:

'I was to make the coffee ready for when you wake up, *Señor* Steele. You went to sleep too soon last night for me——'

'I've gotten used to doing things for myself,' Steele told her, poured himself a cup of coffee.

The girl said, unable to conceal her irritation: 'We try only to repay you for what you do for us.'

Steele experienced the familiar disgust with himself for taking issue with this small girl over such a small thing. He nodded, replied: 'I know. And I reckon we'll be even by the time I get back.'

'You are leaving?'

Steele started for the door, carrying the cup of coffee. He paused to pick up the Colt Hartford from where it leaned against the wall beside the doorway, took his hat and sheepskin coat from where they hung on pegs behind the door.

Garcia started to talk in rapid fire Mexican-Spanish and the tone of his voice and his subject caused both girls to pay close attention to him. When he was through they both nodded, spoke terse affirmative responses.

'*Adios, buena suerte, Señor* Steele,' Maria said solemnly. 'That means goodbye and good luck to you.'

Garcia explained: 'I tell my daughters you intend to go to Broadwater, *mi amigo*. Maria says goodbye and good luck. But I think she means *hasta luego*: see you later, uh?'

'*Señor*, if you please!' Maria called when Steele put on his hat, made to step out through the doorway. Then, as he looked quizzically back at the little girl she seemed strangely afraid, began to speak fast to her father in their own language.

Garcia began to nod, then after a few seconds he held up his hand to signal the girl he had heard enough, would do as she asked.

'My younger daughter, *mi amigo*? She says to ask if you will ask after her mother. If there is the opportunity to do this, *señor*?'

'I'll keep it in mind.'

'We can ask nothing more of you, *señor. Muchas gracias.* Should you happen to see her, *por favor*, tell Carmelita no matter what she has done, she is still wanted by her husband and our two fine daughters?'

Maria nodded emphatically, her expression earnest.

When Steele glanced at the older Garcia girl she stayed resolutely with her back toward him, her movements stiff as she filled three cups with coffee: like she did not trust herself to add to the plea, maybe afraid she might break down into tears for the first time since Steele had started to share in the series of traumatic experiences which had beset her family.

He stepped outside and crossed to the barn. Interrupted the saddling of his riding gelding from time to time to sip at the coffee. Then led the horse out into the sunlight that was as warm as it was bright now the night chill had burned off the land.

He swung up into the saddle, but reined in the animal after just a few strides. Midway from the barn to the track between the crop fields that ran out on to the start of the Timber Creek spur. This when the elder Garcia girl appeared at the open doorway of the house.

She cleared her throat, worked to spread a determined look across her face, promised: 'We will take real good care of this fine place until you bring my *mama* here, *Señor* Steele.'

'That's not why I'm going to Broadwater, young lady,' he told her evenly.

She nodded, shrugged, countered with the opinion: 'I think, *señor*, you are a man who does not always do what he says. And sometimes I think you do not always say what you will do, either.'

Steele showed an expression on his freshly shaved face that was almost rueful, asked: 'How old are you, Conchita?'

'I am almost eight years old, *señor*.' She accompanied this with a knowing smile that gave her face a kind of immature sensuality: suggested she would be far more attractive than her pretty young sister when they had become fully grown women. 'Sometimes it is difficult to believe I am so young, is that not so? I have heard of this before.'

'Yeah.' He made to move the horse forward.

'It has happened since my *mama* went away, *Señor* Steele,' she hurried to explain. 'I have needed to grow up very fast. To take care of my sister, Maria. And in many ways, my *papa*, too. Sometimes, my *papa*, he calls me *poco madre*. That means little mother. Sometimes when I do what must be done, I can be *mandon* . . . you know, bossy? Maybe this is why you do not like the little mother so much, *señor*?'

'Maybe,' Steele growled, heeled the gelding forward, then muttered as his voice became masked by the clop of hooves. 'But right now I don't give too much of a damn about you, miss. More concerned with a big mother.'

9

Adam Steele had the problem straightened out in his mind long before he came down off the bottom of the hill to the south of Broadwater and rode past the town limits marker at the start of California Avenue.

He was back in this town on the lake shore purely to secure his own ends. To square himself with Gavin Fenton, the top hand over the men who worked out of the law office, and to settle the personal score with Whitey Burnett. So, should he ever in the future need to return, be it for business purposes or the pursuit of pleasure, he would be able to do so untroubled by the kind of tension that rode with him today. Or not, as the case may be.

The case this morning was that the family problems of Esteban Garcia and his two daughters were none of his concern. Or so he had decided: he did not even let his mind dwell on this aspect of yesterday's troubles when he rode past the burnt-out wagon and those rotting parts of the carcasses of the burros that still remained on the trail beside the river since the forest scavengers ate their fill in the night.

After the early start from his spread he had ridden north up the winding trail through the broad, timbered valley at an easy pace, and as he moved on to the avenue that was Broadwater's premier residential street, the clocks he heard chiming in some front parlours of the flanking houses marked the hour of ten.

At this time in the morning there was only light traffic on the broad thoroughfare and the cross streets that intersected California between Front and Pacific. Horseback riders, wagons and a few mostly elderly men and women on foot: people taking the breeze-cooled air or going peacefully about their various business.

Some of the local citizens greeted the Virginian with a nod, a raised hand or occasionally a cheerfully-spoken word. Many more ignored his passing. But he saw nothing in the attitude of this latter group pointedly designed to make him feel a known troublemaker not welcome in Broadwater on this fine summer morning.

The house of the late Porter S. Calendar looked much the same as when he and Rufus Grimes left it last night: except that the notice of the sale of household effects had been replaced by one that proclaimed that the house was for sale.

Yet again the Virginian felt familiar irritation with himself: when he consciously tried to sense watching eyes at the windows of the Falls house. But the building appeared to be as empty of human presence as the one set back next to it.

Further along the street he heard children's laughter and their shrill voices from the play yard of the schoolhouse down a side street: realised the promiscuous Dolly Falls was likely to be a student at the school. And this thought triggered in turn a pang of guilt as he recalled how he had allowed himself to sink to her level of off-colour talk in their exchange last night. And the next moment his mind was crowded with images of the even younger Garcia girls who, in their different way, had gotten to him, too.

'Damn kids,' he muttered, not meaning his voice to be so loud.

An elderly lady, shading herself from the morning sun with an open parasol as well as a broad-brimmed bonnet, smiled as she misheard him, wished him good morning.

Short of the two mansions behind high walls that flanked the northern end of California Avenue, before it became the open trail which led eventually to San Francisco, Steele tugged over the reins to steer the gelding on to Fourteenth Street. Headed west toward the slightly breeze-rippled lake. Halted the horse a hundred feet back from the intersection of Fourteenth with Front, between a Quakers' meeting hall on

103

his right and a Chinese laundry on his left.

Four men had appeared at the corner on the left. Now sauntered forward until they were strung out across the end of the street, obviously putting into effect a pre-arranged plan to block his way. Aware of his arrival in Broadwater, kept informed of his measured progress along California Avenue, told of his decision to turn on to this particular side street.

'You know what you've done, don't you, Steele?' Whitey Burnett said evenly, came to a halt, turned to face the Virginian. He had been first to show at the other end of the laundry from where Steele reined in the gelding, so was the last to reach his position in the line, close to the other corner of the street, formed by a drugstore next to the meeting hall.

'If I don't, I reckon I have no need to worry about it,' Steele countered. Swept his gaze along the line of four men who all faced him now, thumbs hooked over their gunbelt buckles, features set in narrow-eyed, mean expressions not shaded by their hat brims from the bright sunlight at this time in the morning.

'You got plenty to worry about,' the man who stood next to Burnett corrected. He was a head shorter and a lot lighter in weight than the man with white hair. One of the two who had carried Burnett back into the Blue Moon Saloon after Steele knocked him down yesterday afternoon.

The one beside him—a tall, thin individual with a ridged scar on his jaw—had helped with that chore.

'See, I don't know what I've done that particularly bothers you fellers,' Steele drawled as he completed his study of the fourth man: barrel chested, pot bellied, black moustached and in the same mid-thirties age group as the others. He had been in the hotel lobby yesterday, when all the men then had been as elegantly dressed as their women. Today they wore Western garb, complete with the gunbelts and tied down holsters. 'But I guess I'm going to be told?'

'Right!' the scar-faced man said.

'You took a wrong turn, Steele, that's what you did wrong,' Burnett expanded.

'I did?' he shook his head, like he was genuinely puzzled. 'I thought the law office was up here on the north side of town?'

'You should've kept headin' north, outta town,' the man with the beer belly drawled, the Deep South and no education in his voice. 'But you made the turn, so that means you made a mistake.'

'Gonna be a painful one, Steele,' Burnett went on, raised a hand from his belt to tug at his kerchief. Turned his head to the side to ensure that the bruise across his throat was clearly visible. 'Maybe even a fatal one, it could turn out.'

He faced squarely to the front again, dropped his right hand back down to hook the thumb over the gunbelt buckle.

Steele was now fully recovered from surprise at seeing the quartet of men. Knew by their attitudes they had not seen any trace of unease in back of his customary impassiveness, so maybe he had not shown any. Now he consciously worked to maintain the nonchalant posture astride the gelding, while in back of the façade he got ready to respond to whatever move was about to be made against him.

At the same time, he tested his sense for being covertly watched by hostile eyes: thought it likely Burnett would have more than three guns available to back his play. And the others might be in hiding behind him or in the flanking buildings.

He listened to an odd brand of sudden silence in back of a small body of unobtrusive sound. For stretched seconds did not recognise the cause of it, until he isolated the hissing of steam from behind the misted windows of the Chinese laundry. Recalled that before Burnett spoke this had been counterpointed by the sing song voices of the oriental workers in the place.

From elsewhere in this town which did not begin to rip and roar until midday, the only sound he identified was a regular squeaking: probably a sign as it swung in the breeze off Lake Providence.

'You have something in particular lined up?' Steele asked. Did not entirely trust the absence of signals from his sixth sense.

'You bet your lousy ass I have,' Burnett growled, his tone as

105

harshly ugly as the look on his square-shaped, heavily-lined, deeply-burnished face.

'You tell the sonofabitch, Whitey!' the skinny man beside him urged.

'I'm tellin' him, Kildene,' Burnett snarled, spared a part of his scowl for the man.

But Kildene failed to see this since he was staring fixedly at Steele, a look of sadistic anticipation on his emaciated features.

Then Burnett stepped forward and this was obviously a signal in the pre-arranged plan to gain revenge over Steele. For Kildene, the scar-faced man who was taller but thinner, and the one with the beer belly all dropped their right hands, dropped the butts of their holstered revolvers.

Even the hiss of steam under pressure seemed to diminish now. So the regular squeaking of the sign's hinges became the most dominant noise in this section of Broadwater.

'What I'm gonna do, Mr Adam friggin' Steele of friggin' Trail's End,' Burnett said with a grin, rasping the words through clenched teeth, his lips hardly moving, his eyes starting to screw up in the bright sunlight as he moved another step forward. 'What I'm gonna do, is fill you full of regret. For what you done to me yesterday. After I tossed that stinkin' greaser outta Mr Channon's place. And before I could teach that little snot-nosed kid of his a lesson in manners.'

Now Steele was certain he was being watched by eyes other than those of the men aligned across the end of the street in front of him. But the need to concentrate his attention on Whitey Burnett and his three partners was so demanding he had no time nor opportunity to look out for other possible sources of danger.

And, anyway, if he was out-numbered by more than the odds he could see spread out before him, this showdown was already lost. So he thought for only a moment more about watching eyes, decided to assume they were not hostile. A bunch of nervous Chinese, peering from the laundry? Some Quakers cowering in the meeting hall? Or, could be some

California Avenue rich gathered to relish a little vicarious excitement: peering eagerly down Fourteenth from the intersection.

'What do you say about that, Mr Horse's Ass Rancher?' Burnett demanded, his confidence growing by the moment.

The other three men shifted their right hands away from the butts of holstered revolvers, hooked the thumbs over their belt buckles again.

Steele stayed impassively silent.

The man with the beer belly laughed, ended it abruptly to taunt with a sneer: 'Seems like the cat's got his tongue, don't it, Whitey?'

Burnett asked harshly: 'That right? That what happened, Mr High and Mighty buddy of the poor downtrodden Mexican *peons*?'

He directed a globule of saliva into the dust four feet in front of him.

Steele said: 'Mostly I just talk when I have something to say.'

Burnett spread a brutal grin across his face. Slowly moved his hands a short way, unbuckled his gunbelt. Challenged as he held the belt to his waist with his left hand, dropped the right to unfasten the holster toe ties from around his thigh: 'So? Okay, what would you have to say if I told you I don't figure you got enough space to spare inside? To fill you with all that regret for what you done? Little man who figures he's such a big shot? First I got to knock all kindsa shit outta you to make room? What you have to say now, uh?'

The short and skinny man at his side giggled.

Burnett let go of the gunbelt and it fell in an arc on the dusty ground at his heels. He took another step forward, away from the belt, demanded: 'I said, what would you say to that?'

'Just you going to do it?' Steele asked evenly, hitched the reins over his saddlehorn.

'Certainly just me, pint size!' Burnett gestured with a sideways jerk of his head. 'Don't you mind these jokers. Kildene and Conner and Brady are around to make sure you don't come up with no more of them sneaky tricks, that's all. Like the one we heard from old John York you pulled on them Red Dog boys at old John's livery last night.'

'I'm relieved to hear that,' Steele said. Made moves like he was about to dismount: withdrew his right foot from the stirrup, put his gloved left hand on the saddlehorn wound with the reins.

The tall man with the scar, who had nodded grimly when the name Conners was spoken, vented a harsh laugh, blurted: 'Relieved is sure what you'll be after Whitey gets through with you! When you had all that shit knocked outta you, uh?'

Up until this moment Steele was undecided: still considered playing it Burnett's way. Trust that in the middle of the morning in a law-abiding town like Broadwater the unwritten rules of the street brawl would be strictly applied. Which probably meant that, up against the much taller and heavier man, he would get badly beaten: and no more than this.

But the risk of trusting men such as these to leave the matter like that was too great to take. So he made his decision. In a stretched second abandoned the slow dismount. Switched into a series of fluidly fast actions which was certain to provoke violent retaliation from the Broadwater men.

And so it was.

He dropped down into the saddle, swung his right foot back into the stirrup, slid the Colt Hartford clear of the boot. And Kildene, Conner and Brady suddenly stopped grinning, vented enraged snarls as they streaked their right hands from the belts at their bellies, reached for their revolvers. At the same moment, Burnett uttered a strangled cry of shock, took a long step backward to put himself behind his discarded gunbelt.

By then Steele was firmly in the saddle astride the uneasy but unmoving gelding: the Colt Hartford aimed from his shoulder, hammer back. And, without compunction, he triggered a bullet into the narrow chest of Conner, the fastest on the draw. Then he raked the rifle to the left, thumbed back the hammer. Blasted a second shot into the centre of Brady's fleshy face.

The little man went down like a felled tree, his hand still fisted tightly around the butt of the revolver that remained in the holster, blood gouting from the single hole where his nostrils had been. Was sprawled out on his back moments before Conner went down. For the taller man, a bright stain blossoming across his chest, staggered several paces in an ungainly backward run before his muscles surrendered in the struggle to keep him upright and he flopped into the dust like a loosely filled sack.

Steele was vividly aware of the acrid stink of black powder smoke, clearly heard the echoes of the two shots resounding between the flanking buildings, felt the blood pumping from his heart to his brain with surging force.

He swung the rifle through an arc to the right, cocked the hammer. But was able to stay his fingers on the trigger while he peered at Kildene, seemingly through a kind of red haze that shimmered in the bright sunlight, reflected off the blood that had welled up from the wounds of the two dead men.

Kildene stood with his feet wide apart, his arms thrust skywards, hands clawed, his mouth gaping. Perhaps he shrieked as soon as his mouth snapped open when he stared in horror at the smoking muzzle of the rifle that came to bear on him. Or maybe there was a time delay. It seemed so to Steele as he heard the shrill cry: '*NOOOoooo!*' ring out like it was another echo from deep within an enormous cave.

The Virginian shifted the aim of the rifle again. Swung it toward Whitey Burnett. Who was down on his haunches, reaching forward with both hands: one to steady the holster, the other to slide the Colt from it. Steele aligned the sights of the Colt Hartford at the small bald patch within the circle of thick white hair. Clear to see because Burnett's hat had fallen off in his haste to go down for his gun.

'Don't be a crazy fool, Whitey!' The shrillness had disappeared from Kildene's voice. He sounded suddenly hoarse.

Burnett jerked up his head, the scowl of fury on his face

immediately changing to a look of pure terror when he found the rifle now aimed at the bridge of his nose. Across a hundred feet or more. Which range he maybe took into consideration for part of a second. Before he wrenched his head to the side, saw Kildene with his hands clawed at the air as if fastened in a grip on the intangible.

Then Burnett glimpsed the bodies of Conner and Brady, transfixed by death against the hard-packed dirt of the intersection, the spurts of blood from their wounds now diminished to trickles. He was starting a double-take at the corpses when Steele exploded a third shot from the Colt Hartford.

The squatting man snapped his head around again. Confused for several moments, like he found it difficult to comprehend why he did not feel the impact of the bullet through his flesh. But then he saw the angle at which the rifle was aimed from Steele's shoulder. Looked down at the ground, saw the gunbelt which he had released a moment before had been blasted two feet back from where it had been lying.

'You bastard, you killed my buddies,' he accused, his voice croaking.

'That's a truth I can't deny, feller,' Steele said. Lowered the Colt Hartford until it was levelled from his hip, still aimed at Burnett as he snatched up his hat, jammed it on his head, rose slowly to his full height. 'As a line shooter I'm not so hot. But with this rifle I reckon I'm pretty damn good.'

From behind him Steele heard a vaguely familiar voice ask in a slightly taut tone:

'You people about through disturbing the peace of this town?'

Steele had sufficient confidence in Sheriff Gavin Fenton to slide his thumb off the hammer, slope the barrel of the Colt Hartford up to his shoulder before he turned his gaze away from Burnett and Kildene, looked behind him.

Fenton, Luke Dexter and a third man, each of them with a silver star pinned to his shirt front on the left, had stepped out of the alley between the Quaker meeting hall and a gunsmith store. All the lawmen packed holstered Colt revolvers, carried Winchester rifles angled across their chests, muzzles aimed at the cloudless sky, fingers hooked through the levers.

'This out-of-towner just shot my two good buddies, Mr Fenton!' Burnett snarled, the huskiness of fear gone from his voice so he again sounded hard and mean. 'You knew Lester Conner and Nick Brady?'

'I saw the whole thing,' Fenton said flatly.

He was a six footer who probably weighed a solidly packed two hundred pounds. Broad shouldered, narrow waisted, with legs that looked to be a couple of inches longer than they should have been for perfect proportion. He was pushing fifty, had a face that was inscribed with a hundred lines for every year he had lived. It was square shaped, burnished by the outdoor life, topped by greying and thinning curly hair. In repose his features looked almost gentle, like he was a man without a mean fibre in his being. But such a man would not be able to enforce the law in a town like Broadwater.

'All I planned to do was pay the bastard back for what he done to me, damnit!' Burnett snarled, wrenched the kerchief from around his neck to display the mark of yesterday's violence across his throat. 'There wasn't any call for gunplay!'

'I heard about yesterday's trouble,' Fenton said in his easygoing voice as he and the deputies who flanked him came to a halt alongside Steele's gelding.

'Me and Nick and Lester, we was only along to see fair play, Mr Fenton!' Kildene defended, lowered his arms until his hands, clenched into tight fists now, were level with his shoulders. 'When he pulled out that fancy rifle against Whitey, after Whitey'd disarmed himself, well we had to go for our——'

'I said I saw the whole thing,' Fenton broke in, a note of impatience in his voice. 'Which is over now. Unless any of you men haven't had enough of killing yet?'

He raked his eyes, which were green tinted, back and forth between Burnett and Kildene. And the two men looked sullenly chastened as they shook their heads.

'What about you?' the sheriff demanded as he looked up at

111

the mounted Virginian. 'You still hungry for more gunplay, mister? Or is this duel ended?'

The Virginian lowered the rifle from his shoulder, turned it and pushed it back into the boot. Replied evenly: 'Enough is enough, sheriff. Since to hear you tell it, I've already had seconds.'

10

The Broadwater law office and jailhouse was an L-shaped building of red brick on Front Street, midway between Twelfth and Thirteenth. The office faced out across the lake, the block of six cells ran back toward California Avenue, with a wagon-wide alley between it and the blank side wall of the Lucky Seven Casino. So miscreants who found themselves languishing in the cells could probably hear the noise from the casino coming in through the barred windows, but were unable to watch those more fortunate than themselves who were still free to indulge in the pleasures of gambling.

Steele knew of the building and had formed this opinion of one aspect of it, from passing it on previous, less eventful visits to Broadwater. For several minutes in the wake of the latest trouble with the men from the Blue Moon Saloon, he could not be sure if he was going to have an opportunity to check if his assumption was correct.

For after Gavin Fenton had ordered Burnett and Kildene to haul the corpses of their former partners to Chambers Funeral Parlour, told Dexter and the red-headed deputy, named Rawlings, to continue their routine patrols, he asked Steele to get down from his horse, take a stroll around to the law office.

But although it had been couched in the form of a request, Steele knew it would be foolish to decline the invitation. For there was a tacit but clearly defined strength of purpose underlying what the lawman had said. It was just a beat away from being an order.

Steele had agreed with a nod, swung down from his horse as the noise from the Chinese laundry increased to its former level and many more sounds of the town made themselves heard. Then he was as comfortable with the lack of conversation as was the laconic sheriff during the easy stroll to the end of Fourteenth Street, then south on Front.

A dozen or so people greeted the lawman respectfully, were acknowledged with curt nods. The same people eyed Steele surreptitiously with a gamut of expressions ranging from intrigue to something akin to pity.

Fenton went in through the doorway between two windows hung with lace curtains, left Steele to hitch the gelding to the rail across the sidewalk. When the Virginian entered the office, the Colt Hartford sloped to his shoulder, Fenton was in a rear corner, replacing the Winchester in a rack.

'Like you to know I was on my way to see you when the trouble started,' Steele said. Chose not to remove his hat and hang it on the stand beside the doorway where Fenton had lodged his Stetson—sombre-hued and a little the worse for wear like the rest of the outfit.

The lawman dropped into the padded swivel chair behind a scuffed and scarred but tidily organised desk, gestured for Steele to take the less comfortable ladder-backed chair in front of it.

The desk and its attendant chairs were the dominant features of a large room with whitewashed walls, pleasantly shaded at this time on a summer morning. There was a row of four more chairs, mismatched and more suitable for kitchen furniture, along the wall to the right. Against the wall to the left, next to the rifle rack, was a pot-bellied stove in which the last fire had long since gone out, and beside this a substantial looking safe. The door to the cells was in the centre rear and on one side of this the wall was hung with wanted flyers: some discoloured and curled with age, others fresh off the press. To the other side were framed clippings cut from newspapers. Steele guessed these were accounts of Fenton's past triumphs in the upholding of law and order in town.

114

The lawman now clasped his hands together on the desk top, interlocked the fingers and stared hard at them: like they had a will of their own and he dared them to disengage before he was good and ready. Replied to the Virginian's opening gambit: 'Like you to know something, too. That I don't tell lies, Steele.'

'I say you did?' Steele was puzzled, ready to get angry.

'I told you people up on Fourteenth: I was there. Saw everything, from the start of the trouble. So then, I heard you tell them boys of Channon's you were heading for this office, didn't I?'

Steele made the effort to contain his irritation with the even spoken, supremely confident man: prepared to explain further. But Fenton raised his gaze from his hands, directed it full into the Virginian's face in a way that commanded he stay quiet until the point was made.

'I'm not going to try to get cute with you, Steele. I'll tell you right off, I've heard a bit about you. Officially—in a manner of speaking—from Sheriff Len Fallows. Who I know you're not exactly on best of terms with? And some other folks. From Providence and here in this town. Heard enough to figure you're either a natural born troublemaker, or the natural born sort of man that draws trouble. Like a flame draws moths. Or a privy flies.'

He pulled his hands apart, held up one as if he expected to be interrupted. Was surprised when it never happened. Then grinned briefly before he frowned: 'Hell, I said I wasn't going to get cute with you, didn't I? So let me put my cards down on the table. Since I know you, I figure you know me? You being the kind of man I know you to be? If you see what I mean?'

Steele said: 'If that's a card on the table, it's face up.'

'Yeah. Way I'm going to deal the whole pack.' He clasped his hands on the desk top again. 'Broadwater's a different kind town to Providence. The kind of trouble they've had down there since you moved in on the old Sanderson place . . . Well, I wouldn't tolerate that getting started here in Broadwater. If I did, the kind of town it is, every itchy-fingered gunslinger, cheating gambler, eye-for-a-fast-buck

115

whore and all kinds of carpetbaggers and Johnny Come Latelies of that nature would move on in. Soon as they knew there was weak law here.

'So I never let that kind of trouble do more than raise its ugly head without I stamp on it real fast, real hard. As the man behind the badge. Legal. You get my drift?'

'Sure, they're still showing face up.'

'Right.' Fenton nodded emphatically, relishing having what he said understood at the first telling. 'And I stay on top of things around here by keeping my finger on the pulse of this town, so to speak. If anything goes on in Broadwater I don't know of in advance—or find out about pretty damn soon after it happens—then it's not against the law. And it doesn't constitute incitement to break the law.'

Gavin Fenton was the kind of pipe smoker who enjoyed tobacco for pleasure rather than as a habit. He made a ritual out of the practice, which he now started to perform. Carefully took all the necessary paraphernalia from a drawer of the desk, hardly interrupted the flow of his talk while he checked the stem was not blocked, tamped tobacco into the bowl, struck a match and drew against the pipe until it burned evenly. The smoke smelled good.

'I knew you were in my town yesterday, Steele. Looking for Rufus Grimes, so looking to buy some bargain furniture for the old Sanderson place. I heard about how you laid out Whitey Burnett before he could knock the block off that Mexican kid. Later, how you handled the card game with Benson and his crowd at the Red Dog. Kept the money you won fair and square when they came after you to get it back. I even know how you beat down Rufus Grimes after he and the Bonney woman tried to cheat you over prices for poor old Porter Calendar's furniture.'

He smiled, highly satisfied with the scope of his information.

Steele said sardonically: 'If you keep your finger much tighter on the pulse of this town, you could throttle it.'

Fenton broadened his grin to show pleasure, teeth clenched to the stem of the pipe. 'Yeah, I could do that. Easy

116

as you could have throttled Buddy Benson in old John York's livery stable last night. But I guess we're both men who know just how far to go, uh?'

Steele countered flatly: 'I'll go as far as necessary to keep from getting killed, Sheriff.'

Fenton nodded. 'That's fair enough, Steele. If all else is equal and it's not you who set yourself up to get killed so you have the excuse to claim self defence. I figure those Blue Moon boys might have killed you just now. Burnett if you'd got into a fist fight with him. Or, way it turned out, if you weren't so handy with that fancy rifle Abe Lincoln made a present of to your Pa?' The lawman was still enjoying the far-ranging extent of his knowledge.

Steele ran a thumb over the inscribed gold plate screwed to the right side of the fire-scorched rosewood stock of the Colt Hartford, the inscription reading: *'To Benjamin P. Steele, with gratitude, Abraham Lincoln.'*

Fenton went on with a rueful shake of his head: 'Yeah, it's likely any one of those three trigger happy gunslingers would have blasted you into the Promised Land if you'd happened to beat Burnett in a fist fight. Or you weren't so fast with that rifle. Which is why you're sitting here shooting the breeze with me. Instead of kicking your heels in one of the cells out back, waiting for the next session of the circuit court.'

He removed the pipe, set it carefully down in a metal ashtray, balanced so the hot tobacco embers did not spill out of the bowl. Held up one big hand, counted off the points he made by folding a finger at a time into a fist.

'One, in my opinion Luke Dexter was too damn eager to run you out of town last night, Steele. But I haven't hauled him over the coals over it. Because he didn't know you: didn't understand that what he did was give you an open invitation to come back in. So, two: I knew you'd be back to straighten yourself out with the law here. Three, I heard about what happened to that Garcia family out on the trail. Damn awful thing, but my jurisdiction finishes at the town limits marker south end of California Avenue. Four, if you had come back here to take up issue on the matter of those Mexicans, you'd

117

surely now be cooling off on a cot in one of the cells. Five . . .'

He tucked the thumb inside the fist, opened his hand, clenched it more firmly than before. 'You break any laws within my jurisdiction, I'll get you for it. And if any of them laws happen to be capital offences, I'll be as happy to watch you swing from a rope as any other fast-shooting trouble-maker comes to this town and goes wrong. If that's the sentence passed on you by the circuit judge. We understand each other still, Mr Steele?'

'I think we speak the same language, Sheriff,' Steele said, having noted the title placed before his name this time. 'Plain and simple.'

Fenton nodded, picked up the pipe, drew steadily on it to get the fire going again. Took the stem out from between his teeth to say: 'Always figured a man who dresses something up fancy, then he's either not sure of his ground, or he's trying to be cute to the man he's talking to. So, Mr Steele, consider the order to get out of town rescinded. Come back here as often as you like. But keep your nose clean, wherever you go, uh?'

The Virginian nodded.

'And I mean wherever you go. Keep it in mind it wasn't just me and my deputies knew you were back in town this morning. Knew where you were every step of the way until those Blue Moon hoodlums tried to stop you going any further. I don't play fear nor favour in how I keep the peace in this town, but there are certain winds that blow . . . well, I sometimes have to bend to them a little.'

He looked discomfited for the first time. Then clenched the stem of the pipe firmly back between his teeth in a way that signalled he considered the exchange was at an end. On a law business level, anyway.

Maybe, as he again began to smoke the pipe in content-ment, Gavin Fenton would have consented to discuss the weather, how the lake fish were or were not biting lately, the political situation in Washington, the price of prime beef, fine whiskey and good quality Stetsons or perhaps his grand-children, if he had any.

In fact, Steele did not know whether the lawman was even

married or not. Which didn't matter a damn here and now. Just as it didn't matter Steele did not know which subjects were of interest in the man on the other side of the desk. For he sure as hell was not here to make small talk about anything. What he needed to do now that the pragmatic lawman was through talking was to ask questions raised by what Fenton had said. To find out if he really had implied what Steele had chosen to infer.

But instead, the Virginian rose from the chair. Picked up the rifle which had been resting against the side of his chair, sloped it to his shoulder. Started for the door. Because, just as there had been an order underlying the request for Steele to come to the law office, so he now sensed there was a tacit warning that Gavin Fenton was in no frame of mind to expand on any of the plain and simple facts he had stated. This discernible from the slight change in his tone, a tightening of the line of his jaw, when he had referred to the certain influences to which he had to respond.

In different circumstances, in another place, Adam Steele would certainly not have left the matter as it lay. Left the office, to step out into the bright day. Where the midday sunshine was reflected off the lake, now mirror smooth since the breeze had stopped blowing across from the hills to the west of the expanse of water.

It had never been Steele's way to back off from a problem: especially when the solution was right there in front of him. But times had changed. He had caused them to change, by choosing to surround himself with the trappings of civilised society. And so he had to abide by the rules that enabled such a society to exist.

Some of the damn rules, anyway!

He unhitched the gelding from the rail out front of the law office. Looked balefully in both directions along Broadwater's main street, which was starting to come to life. Horses and wagons moved steadily back and forth, people strolled the sidewalks and noise emanated from within the many and varied places of entertainment and commerce that lined the double curve of the lakeside thoroughfare.

He dodged traffic, led his horse by the reins across to the other side of the street. Stood on the hard-packed ground at the fringe of the sandy beach where no family groups picnicked today. Maybe because it was still too early, or the chill morning breeze had kept people away.

A mangy looking grey dog moved along the beach on an irregular zig-zag course, his muzzle close to the ground. So eager to stay on the trail of what interested him that it seemed likely he was on the scent of a bitch in heat. When he had scampered out of the Virginian's angle of vision, there was just an unmoving, deserted landscape of beach, lake, hills and sky to be scanned. But because of the increasing traffic on Front Street, the loudness of competing sounds from the buildings on the other side, it was not possible for Steele to forget he was still in Broadwater. Where a boastfully proud sheriff maintained the law and order necessary to a civilised society pretty well: except he was ashamed to admit he needed to make compromises sometimes, to accommodate one particular citizen who had the power to make him bend the rules.

Robert C. Channon.

Who Fenton had mentioned in passing, when he referred to Burnett, Kildene and the late Conner and Brady as 'those boys of Channon's.'

Steele knew the full name of the man: even that the middle initial stood for Casper. Which kind of knowledge was nothing special. For there could be few people in Broadwater, the entire length of the Providence River Valley and over a lot of miles in any direction who did not know the name of the man who owned the Blue Moon Saloon, a number of less palatial pleasure emporiums, a bank and a dozen or so stores throughout the town. Also held the mortgages on a great many properties he did not own. And who was rumoured to be the richest, so the most powerful, man outside of the trade, commerce and industry barons up in San Francisco. With whom he rubbed shoulders at the best places whenever he travelled north to the city on the bay.

The man who, Steele knew, he would need to square himself with if he was truly to secure those ends for which he had returned to this town.

'You're Adam Steele, aren't you?'

The Virginian turned away from the deserted beach, the placid lake and the inert hills under the cloudless western sky. Scanned the crowded, noisy street that was at the other extreme of this pastoral peace. Altered the focus of his eyes, to blur the backdrop of the far side of Front Street, the traffic passing to and fro across it. Looked at the badly-dressed young woman with dishevelled hair, an angular face and a scrawny body as she halted a buckboard alongside him.

'So I know your name?' she rasped, an expression of deep unease suddenly spread across her dirt-smudged and sweat-beaded features. 'That any call for you to stare at me so mean, mister?'

Since he had settled at Trail's End, Steele had taken to smiling a lot more than he used to. When he was not smiling his expression in repose was as a rule pensively impassive. Now, for the first time in a long time, he was made aware that his facial muscles had pulled his features into the shape of the ugly scowl that was first manifested during the War Between the States. Then had fastened a grip on his face in numerous dangerous circumstances while he rode the harsh trails through the violent peace. Very infrequently, when the trouble that came to him—*like flies to a privy* was Fenton's phrase that stuck in his mind—at Trail's End, were of the worst possible kind, he had looked the kind of glowering ogre he realised he must now appear to the disconcerted woman on the buckboard.

'It has nothing to do with you, ma'am,' he said to her, tipped his hat. Worked to rid his face of the evil expression that had come to it unbidden as he peered across the lake: pondered how he had risked a beating, a spell in the Broadwater jailhouse and maybe death, yet still was not certain if he was free to walk the streets of his town in safety: unless Robert Casper Channon ordained that he could. 'I was thinking about something just now.'

The twenty-five-year-old woman, who was dressed like a

121

man, replied on a sighing stream of expelled breath: 'I sure am glad to hear that, mister. You want to ride with me?'

'Just on the buckboard?' he answered quizzically.

She was momentarily puzzled, then righteously angry. Snapped: 'Yeah, sure on the buckboard! I'm not some kind of whore on wheels scouting for customers. I'm Doreen Jones and I have some information you might want to buy. So, do you want to tie your horse on at the back and get aboard?'

He shook his head. 'There's something I need to take care of before anything else, ma'am.'

She peered anxiously to north and south, her narrowed blue eyes paying closer attention to the façades of the buildings immediately across the street, which included the law office. Interrupted the survey to tell him: 'I think that's what I can help you do, mister. But you best make up your mind real fast. Before somebody decides you didn't stop me so you could maybe ask directions to a better place for eating than that grease bowl you were in yesterday.'

Steele looked long and hard at Doreen Jones, thinking of how the men from the Blue Moon Saloon and Gavin Fenton had known so much about his movements in this town. Now he could add to the list this shabby woman who was getting increasingly agitated while she waited for his response.

He checked his own mounting irritation as he asked: 'What's the nature of this information I'm suppose to be so eager to pay for, ma'am?'

'Carmelita Garcia, that's what: or rather, that's who. And...'

She took the time to make another rapid examination of the street in both directions. And Steele felt his face begin to form into another scowl, which probably would not have been so harsh as before. Sufficient to express his anger at being reminded of the Mexican family whose troubles had gotten him into his present predicament.

He was about to snap at Doreen Jones that the wife of Esteban Garcia was not his problem. Until he suddenly had a vivid mental picture of the two small girls at Trail's End: the way they looked at him with their big, round dark eyes when they spoke of their hope he would bring their mother to them. Because of his hesitation, the woman on the buckboard had time to complete her survey, finished what she had started to say:

'... how she got mixed up with that creepy Channon sonofabitch.'

Steele turned to go to the rear of the wagon, said: 'I'll take that ride, ma'am.'

She looked over her shoulder, eyebrows arched in surprise, watched as he hitched the gelding to her rig, asked: 'What'd I say that made you change your mind all of a sudden, mister?'

'Used a magic word,' he said, hauled himself up on to the seat beside her. And glimpsed Gavin Fenton at the open doorway of the law office, looking fixedly across at the rig.

'Magic, uh?' She shook her head, gave a small shrug, grinned sardonically, muttered: 'I been called a bitch often enough before: but never a witch.'

'I'm not calling you any names, ma'am,' Steele said in a matching tone of voice to that of Doreen Jones. 'I'd just like us to talk a spell.'

11

By tacit mutual consent there was no talk as the wagon started forward and Gavin Fenton gripped the pipe between his teeth, withdrew into the law office.

There was much mundane activity on the bustling street as people went about their business, and it was obvious most cared little for concerns outside of their own. For Broadwater was that kind of town, similar to a much larger, overcrowded city in many respects. With many more people, living much closer together, than in a town like Providence.

And this very proximity acted to dissuade the kind of inquisitiveness about other people's affairs that Steele found such an irritant in Providence. Whereas in Broadwater nobody cared about who brushed against him, except to be briefly grouchy at the contact. Such people were most unlikely to pay attention to who rode on the passenger seat of a passing buckboard driven by a less than striking woman. Even if he had taken the trouble to slide his unconventional rifle out of the saddle boot and rested it across his knees.

Unless... It could be there were passers by on the street who considered it best not to notice who rode the wagon. On the principle of what they did not see they could not talk of: or even think about.

'I think we may have gotten away with it, Mr Steele,' Doreen Jones said after the half minute silence between them. Which, he had seen as she appeared to concentrate entirely on steering the rig through the heavy traffic, she actually spent in tense watchfulness.

Which, in turn, he realised with a moment of sour self

anger, had caused him to experience unwarranted high tension out here in the crowded open.

'Everything's quiet, in a manner of speaking,' he said. Managed to create an easy grin as he cupped a hand to his ear, mimed the act of struggling to hear her against the barrage of sound that filled the length of Front Street just after midday. Dropped the grin to ask: 'You said Carmelita Garcia is mixed up with Channon?'

'That's what I said, Mr Steele. But I don't expect any payment for that. Since you must already know it. But I think it's worth some dollars to you to know it's not all her fault. So if you get her away from that creepy sonofabitch, her husband shouldn't blame her for all she's done. Look, that's the place you should eat: over there, back from the corner on Fifth Street. You see it?'

Steele had begun to think he had missed something: that maybe he had only started to give his full attention to Doreen Jones when she was already launched into an explanation of why she was asking for money from him. Yet, at the same time, he felt that if he had opportunity to think about what she said, he would plainly understand exactly what she meant.

Or should he have worked it out for himself? She obviously thought he had.

But he had been preoccupied with the threats, real or imagined, that faced him. At the crudest level from Burnett and Kildene for killing their partners in such humiliating circumstances. While Robert C. Channon would surely not take kindly to having his hired hard men gunned down on the streets of his town. And Gavin Fenton could well be nurturing some resentment for Steele: who had placed him in the invidious position of having to take a public stand against men who worked for Channon.

If he had not spent so much time considering these issues, would he have realised that the severity of the treatment meted out to the Garcia family was motivated by something that went deeper than mere racial prejudice? Which was what Doreen Jones thought he already knew. But, damnit, the missing Carmelita Garcia had not been a priority!

Steele looked across at the place the woman indicated with a hand as she held the horse in the traces of the buckboard steady: waiting for a break in the northbound traffic so that she could make the turn on to Fifth.

It was next to the bakery store on the corner, a two-story, narrow-fronted clapboard building with a window and a glass panel in the door that were as misted by steam as those at the Chinese laundry. A newly painted sign, in vivid crimson on a white background, extended from one side of the building to the other above the window and doorway: THE RED LION CAFE. In the centre of the window and door panel, Steele saw as the woman stopped the buckboard at the sidewalk, were skilfully painted images of mystical looking red lions with fierce eyes and snarling jaws.

'It's my Gramps place,' Doreen said with a hint of pride as she wound the reins around the brake lever. Then she showed an indulgent smile that gave her lean face an appealing prettiness: an expression which suggested how good she could look if she ate a little more, washed off the dirt, smartened herself up. 'And if you think there's nothing so crazy patriotic as an Irishman when he's far from Ireland, you wait until you hear my Gramps after a couple of drinks if somebody happens to make mention of anything Welsh.'

'I didn't take this ride with you to hear about Wales, ma'am,' Steele said, his sudden terseness caused when he looked at the Chambers Funeral Parlour on the opposite corner of Front and Fifth Streets from the bakery and the Welshman's eating house. For, inevitably, he was reminded of the two men he had shot less than an hour ago, who were now over in the granite-fronted building with black velvet-draped display windows showing examples of stark white tombstones and grey crosses.

'You know, you can be a real . . .' She allowed the intended insult to drift away into the hot early afternoon air, permeated on this street by the delicious aroma of newly baked bread. Then she sighed in an animated way that moved her torso to suggest there was more than just skin and bone

126

under the loose-fitting man's shirt she wore with a pair of shapeless blue dungarees. She possessed some pronounced curves that most of the time were concealed by the shirt's check fabric. And Steele was sure Doreen Jones' body would be as good to look at, dressed up, as would her face, made up. She told him: 'But then I guess it's only natural for you to be impatient to get over and done what you came for.'

He decided not to over compensate for his ill humour with the kind of cynical innuendo that had angered her at the outset, confined his response to: 'That's right, ma'am.'

She climbed wearily to the ground and the movements of her slender body again hinted tantalisingly at the pronounced curves within the shirt. Then her choice of phrase acted to keep Steele's thought processes on the same sexual sidetrack when she said:

'I feel kind of naked out here, if you'll excuse me for saying so. But if you want to come inside, it's no lie Gramps and me'll serve you up some grub that'll be a dozen times better than the garbage you had at that grease bowl you were in yesterday at this time. The Shilton couple can talk up a storm, but they can't cook worth a damn. So if you want to eat good while we talk some business?'

Steele took another fast look around. Understood what the woman meant about feeling naked out on this relatively quiet street of this town where he had so many enemies. But he thought he would have chosen to use the word exposed.

When he climbed down from the seat she was already lifting a sack of something heavy off the rear of the buckboard.

'Help you?' he asked.

She shook her head as she balanced the solidly-packed sack on a shoulder, told him a little breathlessly: 'No, not with this meat. But if you want to bring in the box of groceries, I won't give you no argument about that.'

Steele could not carry both the box and the Colt Hartford, so first he crossed the sidewalk with the rifle, opened the door, ushered Doreen Jones inside. Checked over the abruptly silent cafe with a grunt of surprise for what he saw, left the gun propping open the door and went to get the box of provisions.

A burst of rasping talk that erupted while he was at the wagon was immediately curtailed when he re-appeared in the doorway. He set down the box on the nearest table and tipped his hat, smiled with his mouth and picked up the rifle so the door swung closed, greeted:

'Good day to you, ladies. How are things, gentlemen?'

There were five tables in the steamy cafe, the moist air aromatic with the smells of cooking and fresh paint. This line of tables, each with two chairs at either side of them, ran from the misted window to a counter that extended three-quarters of the way across the rear wall of the place. A narrow aisle connected the door to a gap at the end of the counter where Doreen stood beside a slightly-built, watery-eyed, grey-bearded, sullen-looking man of past seventy, maybe eighty, who now held the sack of meat.

The old-timer was confused as he switched the ill-humoured gaze of his grey eyes from the woman, to Steele, to the half dozen customers who had suddenly lost their appetite for food, their thirst for coffee, and interest in the conversations that had briefly been so fast and furious after they saw Steele appear then go from sight.

'Fine with us, how're you doin', Mr Steele?' the lame man who walked with two sticks greeted brightly, ended the silence but hardly reduced the tension at all.

The man who shared a table with Fulton Crabtree hurried to add in a thickly accented voice: 'I am most pleased you were able to come to arrangements with Mr Grimes for the wardrobe, sir.'

Steele recalled that the name of this nervous-looking man was Lars Johannsen.

Mrs Bonney—Grimes' co-conspirator in the attempt to hike the auction prices—sat at a table with three other women of similar late middle age who were unknown to Steele. Urged by the sour-faced Bonney women they now began to whisper among themselves, pointedly did not look at the newcomer once they had conveyed their opinions of him with brief glowers.

'I'm surviving, feller,' Steele told Crabtree. Added in the same even tone: 'I didn't need those clothes from the closet anyway, Mr Johannsen, so it worked out fine for both of us. We all have to raise a little cash the best way we can in these hard times, Mrs Bonney.'

The rifle canted to his shoulder in the usual way, he started down the aisle between the tables and wall hung with gilt-framed paintings of snow-capped or mist-shrouded mountains. The paint on the pictures had been dry a long time. That on the walls and the ceiling was dry, but for only a few hours: still gave off the strong odour that permeated the moist air of the cafe. The steam which had misted up the windows entered the room through a hatch in the wall behind the counter. It and the appetising aroma of boiling ham it carried were now much diminished.

As Steele moved along the aisle he drew a relieved sigh from the Swede, a broad grin from Crabtree, nervous frowns from Mrs Bonney's table companions and a withering glare from the woman herself: like she considered he had insulted her but she was not prepared to take issue with him beyond showing her tacit disdain.

When he sank on to a chair at the table nearest the counter, turned toward the old man who was obviously Gramps, the quartet of women suddenly rose as a group and bustled out of the cafe: their heads high in the air, not looking back, not saying anything. Mrs Bonney was last to leave and she slammed the door with enough force to rattle the glass panel in its frame.

The white-aproned old man with the sack of meat on his shoulder divided a perplexed frown between Doreen and Steele, asked: 'What did I do to you, boyo, that you must come to my cafe, upset my customers to such an extent they leave in such high anger?'

He enunciated his words with great precision, had an accent as lyrical as if he had just got off an Atlantic clipper after a record crossing from his native land.

'He helped me to bring in the supplies you sent me for, Gramps,' the woman with a native American drawl hurried to explain. 'Mr Adam Steele, this is David Jones, my

129

grandfather and known to one and all as Gramps. Gramps, this is Mr Adam Steele.'

'Who is prepared only to help you so far, it looks to me, girl,' the Welshman growled. 'If it prevents him having hold of that rifle of his.'

'I think he's going to eat here, Gramps,' Doreen placated, still on the defensive. 'That'll more than make up for losing those old biddies who just spend hours and hours gossiping over a cup of coffee each. And Mr Steele has good reason to keep his rifle close at hand.'

David Jones looked like he could be getting ready to spit, but in time recalled where he was. Confined himself to a deep-throated grunt of disgust, then countered: 'Do you think I do not know that, girl? Do you think I do not know why decent women rush to get out of the way of this boyo? Just because I am old and weak in the back, that does not mean I am totally deaf and too weak in the head to reason over what I hear. This Adam Steele is in trouble, girl. And I am not pleased you brought him here to my premises. Go to fetch the rest of the provisions, Doreen. Our remaining customers will require dessert soon.'

There was a two-way swing door in the rear wall immediately behind the end of the counter and as the old man spoke he turned, pushed through the doorway with the sack of meat.

The woman made a face after him, then directed a wan look of encouragement at Steele, moved to do her grandfather's bidding.

Crabtree and Johannsen started to eat their good-smelling beef stew again, but with a measured slowness: attempting not to be through before they learned the outcome of this latest development in the Virginian's troubled times.

Doreen paused at the front of the cafe, cleared a space in the condensation. Peered out at the street, showed no reaction to what she saw there, then came back along the aisle. She smiled personally at the slow-eating old men then showed a grimace only Steele could see once she was past them. Said:

'Since Gramps figures your new-found fame means you're more likely to scare folks away than pull them in, maybe it'll be best if you eat out in the kitchen, Mr Steele? The beef stew—that's the special today—or anything else on the bill of fare is just as good to eat out back as in here.'

'Fine with me, ma'am,' he said, rose from the table then paused as he was about to follow the slender, unflatteringly garbed woman through the swing door. This when Fulton Crabtree called:

'You be careful out there, son!' He cackled with laughter. 'Miss Doreen's husband huntin'. And usually it's only the ones she figures are likely prospects that get invited out to the kitchen.'

'I'm grateful for the warning,' Steele said lightly.

Crabtree told him ruefully: 'Weren't a warnin' exactly, son. When Doreen's prettied up instead of havin' them baggy old work clothes hung on her and she ain't dirty and sweaty from doin' heavy work . . . Well, she's the kinda girl I'd have ridden a lot of miles for when I was young.' He shook his head, added with genuine sadness: 'And able bodied, course.'

'Thank you for those few kind——' the woman started to call good naturedly.

Steele looked back as he pushed through the doorway, responded to Crabtree's wink with a grin, made a circle of his thumb and forefinger. Then he went into the kitchen. Killed the grin, broke the approving circle but kept his hand up, away from the Colt Hartford he held down at his side in his other, left, hand, muzzle angled at the floor. This as he saw what it was had caused Doreen to break off in mid-sentence.

The sight of her grandfather with a revolver muzzle pressed into the side of his neck while one of his arms was pushed far enough up his narrow back so he was forced to bend half forward from the waist. The man who held David Jones this way, threatened him with the cocked Frontier Colt, was the big-built, button-eyed Red Dog Saloon man named Billy. The two of them standing near the open rear door through which Billy had obviously just entered.

Billy was not making this play alone. Across from the rear

doorway which was in the far right hand corner of the sparsely but adequately furnished kitchen was the foot of a banistered staircase. Midway down the stairs was the spade-bearded Buddy Benson who aimed a smaller, fancier hand-gun at Doreen.

She stood close to the bottom of the staircase, near a cupboard on which she had set down the box of groceries beside the sack of meat.

A moment after Steele became as still as David and Doreen Jones, the swing door smacked into his back and in another moment was unmoving in its frame.

Billy blinked a great deal, but otherwise did not move.

Benson had paused when Steele came into the kitchen but now continued down the stairs. The gun he kept steadily aimed at the head of the woman was a pearl handled .22 calibre weapon he probably carried in some kind of concealed, spring loaded holster. A gambler's gun, virtually useless outside a longer range than the width of a card table. With each part of a second that elapsed while Doreen and Steele remained voluntarily unmoving and David Jones was forced to be still, the distance between the small gun and its target narrowed.

Benson's brutal grin conveyed his supreme confidence that he was in total command of the situation.

Billy, from his scowl, thought nothing good could come out of what was happening.

When he came down off the staircase, Benson did not allow the little gun to waver as he issued a tacit instruction to Steele with his free hand and a pointed glance. When the Virginian had done what was asked of him—moved along from the door and slid closed the hatch—Benson congratulated in a cynical tone:

'Wise man. And me, too. For figurin' you wouldn't risk the lives of this couple of innocents to save your own skin.'

'Tell him to lay down the damn rifle, Buddy!' Billy urged, soft but harsh, his voice rasping out of a throat dry with fear.

'Yeah, why don't you do that, Steele?' Benson said evenly. 'Just lean it against the wall. And step away.'

He rested the heel of his gun hand on the shoulder of the woman who uttered a strangled cry when the muzzle of the revolver touched the flesh just beneath her right ear.

She was losing the struggle to hide the full extent of her terror, suddenly looked ready to keel over into a faint. But a grunt of pain from her grandfather helped her remain in control of herself.

A log cracked in the range on top of which the pot of cooking ham had gone off the boil, the water steaming hardly at all now.

Benson hardened his tone, warned as the threatened old man and his granddaughter both eyed the Virginian imploringly: 'If you don't do what I said, Steele, the old guy gets his arm busted. Then he gets a bullet in the head. The lovely lady here . . .' He pulled a face that wrinkled his nose as if from a bad smell, 'she just gets a bullet in the head, plain and simple. Plain like she is. Simple as pullin' a trigger. And if them two old crocks out front show up in here, they'll be done for, too. And I wonder who'll get the blame for all that killin'?'

Steele half turned, leaned the Colt Hartford against the wall below the closed hatchway.

'Real wise!' Billy said. And the relief he experienced seemed as great as that felt by David Jones whose arm he released so that the old man could stand upright. Held the gun pressed against his back as he went on: 'You gotta know it wasn't no secret you rode down to this place with the old boy's granddaughter, Steele? So everyone'll figure for sure you did the killin', uh? Stands to reason. Won't be the first time you killed anybody in this town, right?'

Steele stepped away from the wall and the rifle.

Doreen, close to tears that would be mostly of relief if they came, pleaded: 'I'm so sorry, mister. They must've followed us. Seen where we came and then went round back. One was upstairs and the other one outside. Soon as Gramps and me——'

'Right, Miss Smart Lady,' Benson snarled, shoved the gun more firmly into her neck, forced her to crane her head under the insistent pressure. 'And we sure didn't go to all that trouble to stand here listenin' to some brainy plain jane spout off!'

Steele spoke for the first time since he entered the kitchen, asked evenly: 'So why did you do it, feller?'

Before the sneering Benson could reply, David Jones spoke with low-toned vehemence in a language that sounded total gibberish.

'What's that you say, Gramps?' Billy demanded, abruptly disconcerted again.

'I told you in no uncertain terms what I think of you, Billy Small!' the old man answered in the same raspingly vindictive tone. 'You and your partner in this evil. In my native Welsh language, boyo! I would not have Doreen hear such filth from her grandfather's lips!'

Benson snarled: 'You keep yakkin', old man—in any friggin' language—and they'll be your last words. And this little lady won't hear nothin' more from anybody. Dirty or sweet talk!'

He swung his glinting-eyed gaze from David Jones to Steele as the Virginian stopped beside the pine table in the centre of the room. Snapped: 'Our money, that's what we came for, Steele. You oughta have figured that out for yourself.'

'Plus interest, Buddy,' Small reminded. 'Don't forget we want extra for our trouble.'

'Yeah, plus interest, Steele,' Benson agreed. 'For the two times and the double trouble. At old John York's livery and here in this dump. A hundred bucks oughta about cover it: that's double double plus a little extra, uh?' He laughed harshly.

The Virginian said: 'That's not the kind of folding money I usually carry around with me.'

Benson grinned first. Small directed a fast glance at him, smiled nervously. And Steele thought he had an inkling of what they had in mind: which had not involved taking any money off him when they started their play. But Buddy Benson was an opportunist.

Now Steele completed his response, before the spade-bearded man could make the revelation that was supposed to come as a frightening surprise to the Virginian:

'Not usually, like I say. But whenever I come to a wide open gambling town like Broadwater, I always carry a little extra. In case I find a big game, you know? Hide it in my boot. A hundred, and you'll let these good people alone?'

There was a straight-back chair under the table. He pulled it out, lifted his right foot to rest on the wood seat.

'But, Buddy——' Small started, growing nervousness spreading sweat across his forehead and along his upper lip.

'Shut up!' Benson growled, and Steele was sure the avaricious gleam in his eyes confirmed that whatever the pair could get off him would be extra to what they were being paid for the play they were making here. 'Yeah, a hundred will cover it fine.'

'Be for all four of you Red Dog fellers?' Steele asked. 'I don't want to get shaken down by those other two who reckon I cheated in the——'

'Phil Turner and Jacko Buckman ain't got no hand in——' Small started.

'Don't give them a red cent, boyo!' David Jones said raspingly.

'Don't trust them, Mr Steele!' Doreen implored.

They were rewarded with vicious jabs of the gun muzzles.

Benson snarled: 'What did Billy warn you about shootin' off your mouth, you old bastard?'

Fulton Crabtree yelled from the cafe: 'Hey, Gramps! You closed the place up for the day to entertain Miss Doreen's new beau? Me and Lars are about ready for a slice of apple pie now the stew's gone down so good!'

'Shit, we friggin' wasted too much damn time, Buddy!' Small groaned. 'I said we oughta get this thing over and done with right off and get the hell out——'

'You hear me!' Crabtree yelled, louder. And then came the sound of chair legs scraping across the floor, next his footfalls and the accompanying rap of his sticks as he headed along the aisle toward the gap in the counter, the swing door into the kitchen beyond.

'Buddy?' Small pressed his partner insistently.

Benson hooked his free arm around the waist of Doreen and she reacted with a sharp intake of breath. But the spade-bearded man only fastened a more secure hold on her so she could not easily jerk away from the threat of the small gun. Then he snarled softly:

'Gramps, go give them old bastards what they want. One wrong move, though . . . Don't expect you to give a shit about Steele. But your granddaughter won't ever have the chance to make you a great grandpa. Let him go, Billy. Go ahead, Gramps.'

Steele saw the sweat on the faces of Doreen and both men from the Red Dog Saloon. Felt his own pores open to squeeze out beads of salt moisture. This in the two seconds it took for David Jones to realise he could do nothing else but what he was told. While the footfalls and the rapping of sticks against the floor of the cafe got dangerously close to the swing door.

'We should've just done what they wanted us——' Small started tautly.

'Gramps, apple pie for me and my good buddy——' Crabtree began to demand.

'All right, all right, boyos!' David Jones bellowed. 'I am coming with them!'

He took a tentative step away from the gun Small held in his back, then hurried across the kitchen, rubbing the pained arm with his free hand. He came to the table where there was a tray ready loaded with two plates of apple pie and a jug of cream. As he picked this up with trembling hands, a look of hatred became deeply etched into the wrinkled flesh of his face above the beard and he said to Steele:

'Your kind are not fit to live among decent people, boyo. There should be an island in the middle of a great ocean where the likes of you and the other scum you draw to you can be kept separate from the rest of us.'

The softness of his strongly accented voice served to give his taunt more stinging force than a snarling tone. He glanced over his shoulder to direct contempt toward Small who still aimed the Colt at him, and Benson whose smaller gun bore hard into Doreen's neck.

136

Small looked insulted by the abuse, but Benson greeted it with harsh laughter.

Steele said: 'I'm inclined to agree with those two, Gramps. You should watch that mouth of yours.'

He half turned, his foot still on the seat of the chair. Lashed out a vicious side of the hand chop against the neck of the old-timer. Gramps let out a shriek of mixed surprise and pain, staggered sideways, dropped the tray and pitched to the floor with a crash and clatter of the tin tray and smashed china.

At the moment the old man vented the cry Doreen wrenched free of Benson's grip, let out a scream of her own, lunged across the kitchen toward her grandfather on the floor.

Benson and Small were both as shaken by what happened as the woman. And in the fleeting seconds as Gramps went down and Doreen rushed to his aid, they might have started to shoot. Raked the kitchen with fast fire. Killed or maimed Doreen, Gramps and Adam Steele. Then the two old men, both of who could be heard coming toward the swing door as fast as they could move.

But it would have been an act of panic, their trigger fingers working to the dictate of fear. For these were not the kind of men who were killers by nature. Unlike Steele. Who, as he had told Gavin Fenton, was always ready to kill if the situation called for such drastic action.

The knife slid from the boot sheath, then through the gaping slit in the outside seam of his right pants leg.

Doreen, her face a mask of horror at what had happened, her mind in a turmoil of hatred for Steele and concern for her grandfather, probably had no thought of fear for the gun that had been pressed into her neck, nor the more lethal Frontier Colt that Billy Small tracked toward her as she lunged between him and the old man he had been aiming at.

'Oh, my God!' Small shrieked when he saw the knife in Steele's hand. And then, in the manner of a man who was always subordinate to the other, he looked toward Benson for guidance.

Benson was still gripped by shock: probably was as petrified now as the woman had been before she was galvanised into action by the vicious attack on her grand-father from such an unexpected source. But this passed in an instant, and he glowered at Steele: in his eyes a brand of hatred a hundredfold greater than that which Doreen—who was also afraid for the fate of her grandfather—had the spare capacity to feel.

In a flash Buddy Benson recalled the way he had been humiliated in the card game at the Red Dog Saloon. Both physically hurt and humiliated worse at John York's livery. Simmered with ill feeling toward the Virginian throughout last night. And during this day as accounts of what happened to him at Steele's hands circulated through this town where news travelled faster than a quarter horse could gallop. And he saw a way to get even for all of this. Grasped for it. Or maybe, quite simply, he saw Steele as a killer without compunction: sought to strike the first blow. Acted in self defence when he thrust the tiny gun forward, squeezed the trigger.

At the same instant, Steele released the knife with a powerful throw. Dropped down on to his haunches for two purposes. To try to duck under the bullet, at the same time to hook both gloved hands under the pine table.

He achieved just one of his objectives. For the small calibre bullet impacted with his upper left arm as he saw the knife complete its spinning journey, thud into the chest of Buddy Benson. Who staggered back, hit the wall, dropped the little gun, brought up both hands to clutch at the knife sunk deep in his flesh.

By then the table was on its end, formed a shield of sorts between Steele and the man at the kitchen's rear doorway who still had a gun. But it was a less than perfect defence against such a man should Billy Small rush forward, swerve to the side, blast at point blank range at anybody crouched behind the upended table.

It was a reasonable diversion, though, and as Steele suddenly became disconcertingly conscious of the warm moisture on his upper arm, then glimpsed the blood soaking through his shirt sleeve, he took another, greater risk.

Powered himself into a forceful dive, then a roll. Away from the shielding table: out into the open on the other side of it from where Doreen was on her knees, trying to calm Gramps who struggled to stay free of her embraces, snarling a stream of fast spoken words in a mixture of American and Welsh. All of them incoherent, all surely obscene.

Steele's outstretched hand gripped the Colt Hartford. He stayed down, slumped in a half-sitting, half-lying attitude, his shoulder blades resting on the wall, legs splayed across the floor. The base of the rifle stock was braced against his hip as he tracked the barrel. Glimpsed Benson give up the struggle to yank the knife out of his chest, start to slither down the wall between the foot of the staircase and the cupboard, reach blindly for something to support himself. He hooked a hand over the top of the box of groceries, dragged it off the cupboard so that its contents of cans and bottles and packets and paper sacks spilled across the floor. He finished on his haunches. Stared with a mixture of helplessness and hatred at Steele.

Billy Small seemed unable to tear his wide-eyed gaze away from his partner sliding down the wall. But he kept the gun, fisted in a hand trembling with fear or some other equally powerful emotion, aimed in the general direction of the upended table, the people on the floor to either side of it. Then, when Benson sank out of his sight, below the sack of meat on top of the cupboard, he vented a groan, wrenched his head around. Saw Steele on the far side of the kitchen as the Virginian started to rise: one arm run with blood but not so badly hurt he could not keep the rifle levelled, rock steady in a two-handed grip.

David Jones curtailed the profane diatribe.

Doreen cut short her placating words, abandoned her efforts to keep her grandfather down on the floor.

'I reckon you know your friend's the third feller I killed today.' Steele said grimly as the sound of footfalls within the cafe ended. Voices spoke in rasping whispers for a few seconds, then were suddenly silenced. He asked rhetorically: 'I don't reckon you want your number to come up four?'

Steele was aware he was premature about Buddy Benson's end. The man who still squatted on his haunches against the wall at the foot of the stairway was not yet dead. His eyes were staringly wide and unmoving, but the death glaze had not filmed them. Nor was it a muted death rattle that caused the flesh at his throat to pulse. The spade-bearded man was concentrating hard, striving to speak, but not making a sound. He breathed silently through flared nostrils.

Small rasped huskily: 'I want out is all.'

'Drop the gun and take what you want,' Steele invited, eased himself fully upright, but needed to lean his back against the wall.

'You mean it?' Small was incredulous.

Steele nodded. 'I only kill people if they're trying to kill me. Anyway, I reckon I owe you.'

'Uh?' He was more incredulous.

'Last night? In the livery? You didn't know that scattergun of York's wasn't loaded when you stepped in front of it.'

'You must've known I didn't do it to stop you from gettin'——' Small started to blurt, but cut himself short as he realised he was arguing himself out of a favour.

'I know,' Steele allowed. 'But if the gun had been loaded and York fired it, I was one of those he wouldn't have shot.'

Small swallowed hard, directed another sidelong glance toward the cupboard beyond which the dying man was hunkered. For stretched seconds he was mistrustful, then he looked on the brink of tears, before he suddenly pumped his head, opened his hand so the big Colt clattered to the floor.

'Hot damn!' Fulton Crabtree growled as he slid the hatchway open a crack.

Small backed into the open rear doorway, started to turn to leave.

Benson found his voice and his eyes filled with anguish when he tried to yell, could only hiss through clenched teeth: 'Billy, don't! They're gonna——'

There came a barrage of gunfire. Maybe as many as half dozen repeater rifles exploding bullet after bullet into the

140

burly body of Billy Small. Who died on his feet, a look of horror his death mask. Then came staggering into the kitchen on dead legs, propelled by the impact of the hail of bullets tearing into his flesh, blood spurting, oozing, spreading.

But not all the shots found their intended mark. Those that missed cracked through the doorway into the kitchen. Thudded into the floor, the walls, the upended table. Ricocheted off hanging pots and pans. Smashed china stacked on shelves.

Steele, Doreen and David Jones threw themselves flat on the floor, instinctively covered their heads with their arms.

Then there came a sudden silence: except for the gentle hissing of a burning log in the range, the bubbling of the simmering cooking pot, the mass exhalation of breath as those who had survived the fusillade of deadly gunfire expressed their relief at being spared death or injury by a stray bullet.

Buddy Benson, his gaze fixed upon the face down, spreadeagled, bullet-shattered, blood-soaked corpse of his partner said in a hoarse whisper: 'Them Blue Moon bastards killed Billy.'

He shifted his gaze to Steele, raised his voice to ask with sneering contempt: 'How the frig could those crazy sonsofbitches mistake Billy for you?'

Before Steele, rising to his feet, could respond, Gramps who got up more slowly, growled:

'There is little to choose between any of you people close up, boyo. From a distance, just the individual stench of your rottenness is absent, so——'

'That was the play?' Steele cut across the old-timer's embittered voice as he moved to the far side of the bullet-scarred, blood-splattered and crockery-littered room. Did not look at the almost dead man, peered out through the lace curtained window above and to the side of where Benson clung tenaciously to the final threads of his life. Saw a cultivated back yard enclosed by high fences on two sides, the walls of neighbouring buildings on the other two. He

141

paid particular attention to the rooflines of the buildings, failed to spot any sign of movement against the bright afternoon sky. Maybe only thought he heard fast-running footfalls, quickly diminishing into the distance.

'I guess the apple pie's off?' Fulton Crabtree growled, slid the hatch open all the way.

'Don't be such a damned old fool, my friend,' the Swede said earnestly after sneaking a fast, frightened look into the kitchen from the cracked open door. 'We leave now.' He raised his voice as he moved back along the aisle, called: 'We pay for the stew some other time, Gramps!'

Crabtree complained to Johannsen as he left the Red Lion Cafe with the Swede: 'I wasn't bein' serious about the apple pie!'

Nobody offered any response to the two old men.

'That's how it was supposed to be,' Benson replied to the Virginian's query as Steele moved away from him, toward the open rear doorway. Peered out to get a clearer view of the well tended yard, the nearby buildings. 'Whitey Burnett was in the Red Dog. Saw you come outta Gavin Fenton's office and meet up with that girl. Came pretty close to taking a shot at you there and then. But made us the deal instead. Fifty bucks down, fifty more when the job was done.'

'A hundred dollars to kill a man?' Doreen blurted, shocked.

'Such evil men as these can be purchased for much less to do such things, my girl,' her grandfather said.

'Not to kill!' Benson argued adamantly. 'Just to corner you. Let Whitey know where. Fix it so him and a bunch of the Blue Moon boys could take care——'

'Never thought you fellers were the killing kind,' Steele said as he turned from the doorway, went to stoop in front of Benson. Who looked at him with rapidly expanding terror as Steele fisted a gloved hand around the handle of the knife buried in his chest. 'Like to have this back now, okay?'

He jerked the knife free and a little blood squirted out of the wound in the wake of the blade. As a cry that was a mixture of alarm and pain sounded from Benson. Who died a moment later, so did not see the way Steele wiped blood off the blade on the shoulder of his shirt before he replaced the knife to the sheath. Then the Virginian stood up, headed for the rear door, rifle in a double-handed grip so unable to clutch at his bullet-holed arm that had stopped spilling blood, started to pain him.

'My God, how could you do such a brutal thing?' Doreen gasped with a grimace of horror. 'The man was still alive!'

'I have things to do, ma'am. And not much time to do them in I reckon. So no time for wasting.'

'But——'

Steele double checked that the riflemen were gone. Glanced back into the kitchen to growl: 'Sorry about us not being able to have our talk. And some of that fine food you promised. Sorry, too, about slugging you, Gramps.'

He looked pointedly down at the bullet-shattered corpse of Billy Small, added: 'I had to think of something to keep from ending up like him.'

'Sorry doesn't butter any parsnips, boyo,' the old man said, ruefully rubbed his neck where first the gun had been pressed against him, then Steele's blow struck. 'Get your evil carcase off my premises, and don't ever come back!'

'But, Gramps, I feel partly to blame for——' Steele heard the woman start to say with a plaintive note in her voice that was far removed from hatred.

The Virginian stepped outside.

'Silence, girl!' David Jones snapped sternly. Vented a burst of fast talk in his native language, then told her: 'Do not waste your sympathy on such a boyo as he, girl!'

'But he's hurt, Gramps and——'

'Nonsense, girl! He thinks he is a man of iron and there is just one sure way to harm iron!'

'Whatever he is——'

'May he and all his kind rust in peace!'

12

As he stood with his back pressed flat against the wall outside
the kitchen doorway, Steele's sweat-beaded face showed a
grim smile at the old Welshman's sardonic prediction of his
fate. Then grimaced with mixed pain and anger when he
heard a rising volume of shouting on the street out front of
the cafe: suddenly louder as the door of the place burst open.

He could not be sure, but thought he recognised the voice
that made an imperious demand for silence. Sheriff Gavin
Fenton? Who had just happened to be close by when the
shooting started? Keeping his finger on the pulse of
Broadwater?

Then he was unconcerned about the identities of the men
who came through the cafe. He lunged away from the wall,
knew he had to get out of sight before they reached the
kitchen. Heard enough about the killings to bring them
spilling out of the back of the place. As a lynch mob, maybe.
Even if the lawman was one of their number. Unlikely to pay
too much attention to what David Jones and his granddaughter had to say. Inclined, as the two Red Dog Men had
warned, to brand Steele wantonly responsible for both
corpses in the cafe kitchen.

He avoided leaving tracks, did not trample the neat lines of
vegetables growing in the garden. Struggled over a property
fence, his wounded arm hurting worse each time he had to use
it, dropped into the back yard of an adjacent building with a
façade on Front Street, next to the corner bakery.

The noise of pursuit was still confined within the premises
of the Red Lion Cafe. He failed to sense he was being

watched, with hostility or anything else, from the rear windows of any of the surrounding buildings. Was sure the riflemen who killed the hapless Billy Smart were not eagerly watching and waiting for the chance to make good their error.

The yard he was in now was littered with trash: broken-open wooden crates, crushed cartons, the cold ashes of long ago burned out fires on which the lumber and cardboard packages had been tossed.

He picked his way among the litter and the fire detritus, reached the rear door of the building without hearing or seeing anything that caused him sufficient concern to displace diminishing pain and expanding anger.

Just what the building housed he had no idea. He took a deep breath, a firmer one-handed grip on the rifle, tried the door latch. Breathed in the fresh aroma of newly-baked bread which suddenly made him feel sick. Until he discovered with a sigh of relief the latch lifted, the door swung open.

A man said fearfully: 'It's all right, sir. You're safe to come inside. I know what they did to the man they thought was you.'

It was a small, square, windowless storeroom. Piled high with cartons and crates similar to the empty ones outside, plus some bulging sacks. It would have been in total darkness but for the open doorway where Steele stood for a few more moments. Until, as the sound of voices suddenly rose, harsh with righteous anger, he stepped over the threshold. Closed the door quickly but quietly. Made himself as blind as the man on the other side of the room.

Who had not sounded hostile when he spoke. Could have shot down the intruder out of hand when the door opened and Steele was silhouetted against the sunlight that dropped into the rear areas of the surrounding buildings from the early afternoon sky.

As Steele now cut off the light and gave his racing mind time to assimilate the sense as well as the tone of the words he had heard, he saw the man step into sight from behind a ceiling-high pile of crates. Gained the impression of a middle-

145

aged, short and slightly built, bald-headed, red and sweaty-faced man with wire framed spectacles and a bushy grey moustache. Dressed like a storeclerk in a brown overall. Looking afraid but determined to overcome fear. Unarmed, as far as Steele could see from his brief glimpse.

'Best if you slide over the bolts at top and bottom, sir,' the man urged raspingly.

Steele, still stiff with tension and pain, was a little slow to do as he was asked. Stepped back when the man suggested:

'Here, let me: I know exactly where the bolts are. Before that bunch of hooligans come bustin' in here again!'

Aware of the man approaching him through the pitch darkness, brushing against him, Steele registered the word *again*. Then he heard the soft sound of greased metal as the bolts slid firmly home. Knew the unobtrusive noise sounded much louder within the confines of the darkened storeroom than outside. Where voices were raised in a confusing din anyway.

'Like you to leave real fast, if you don't mind, mister,' his benefactor asked anxiously. 'Sorry I can't help you any more than this, but I'm not a brave man, you see. It's just that I'm grateful to you. My way of showin' you that.'

He struck a match, held it high as if primarily to display his nervous frown, his eagerness to be believed. Then he gestured across the room and Steele followed him when he moved off. He looked over his shoulder to check the Virginian was behind him, started to blurt out his reasons for helping a stranger in such a dangerous situation.

'They came here to my store. Told me to make myself scarce, forget they were ever here. But I didn't do that, sir. I hate the men who make Broadwater such a filthy rotten town sometimes. I stayed in my store. And when they came down from upstairs after all the shootin', they threatened me, said if I ever told about them bein' here they'd kill me. Do unspeakable things to my daughter.

'And I won't say anythin' to anyone else, I guess. But I had to do some small thing when I saw they must've made a mistake, saw you comin' this way. I'm glad you did. But I'm scared, too, Mr Steele. So I'd like you to forget you did. Anyway, forget that I helped you.'

Heavy footfalls approached the yard doorway, kicked trash out of the way. Voices sounded. The latch was lifted, the bolted door rattled a little in its frame but remained firmly closed.

'No, the murderin' bastard didn't come this way, Deputy Rawlin's!' Steele thought he recognised the voice of Kildene.

'I told you!' a voice the Virginian failed to connect with a name countered. 'I bet that cold blooded gunslingin' killer beat it down the alley on to Fourth!'

The footfalls and voices retreated as what sounded like a dozen or so pursuers tried to locate the Virginian's line of escape elsewhere.

'You don't have to worry, feller,' Steele told the nervous storeclerk. Removed a glove, explored his shoulder with gently probing fingertips, discovered an entry and exit wound for the small calibre bullet which had penetrated the flesh, maybe chipped a bone, maybe not. 'All I'll say about you is that you're a friend in need. And that just to your face if it's the way you want it. Reckon I can get by without knowing the reason why you're doing this for me.'

The man swore softly as the match burned his fingers, went out: then he halted abruptly so the Virginian bumped into him. But before pitch darkness returned Steele saw they were at another doorway, in the opposite wall from where he had entered the storeroom.

'My name is Falls, sir. Howard Falls. I heard from a friend of your meeting with my brazen daughter yesterday. Before the sale of chattels at the Calendar House. I want you to know I appreciate the way you dealt with her. There have been such goin's on in my house since Dolly's dear mother passed away, God rest her soul...

'Well, that is neither here nor there in the present circumstances. But I surely appreciate your attitude, sir. A man like yourself, if you'll excuse me sayin' so. I also appreciate your stand against the men who make this town the kind that encourages young girls like my Dolly to go wrong. Appreciate it whether you attempt to pursue that matter or whether you choose to leave this town as soon as you are able...

'I know what I would do in your place, sir. But whatever happens, I will sleep more content in my bed, be able to worship at my church with an easier conscience, than I would have been able to. After submittin' to the wishes of those Blue Moon Saloon hooligans who commandeered my premises for their own evil ends. Good luck to you, sir. And may God bless you.'

Falls pushed the door open, ushered Steele out into a haberdashery store, which a sign on the glass-panelled door to the street indicated was closed. The store was half in bright light, half in shade, for the time was now almost one o'clock and the west-facing display windows caught the available afternoon sun at the start of its slow slide down the dome of cloudless sky above the still placid Lake Providence.

'My goodness, you're hurt!' Howard Falls exclaimed as he followed Steele through the doorway into the store.

They were behind a stretch of counter piled high with displays of wool, yarn, paper patterns, fabrics and other paraphernalia of the haberdasher's trade.

'It's one of the hazards of the trade I thought I'd gotten out of, Mr Falls,' the Virginian said, started across the store in which there was some disarray he guessed was caused by the killers of Billy Small as they left after exploding the hail of gunfire from the floor above the store.

Then he ducked behind a display of coloured yarns as footfalls rapped on the sidewalk boarding immediately out front of the store, men's voices rumbled, expressing conflicting opinions as to which way Steele had made his escape from behind the Red Lion Cafe.

'Oh, my goodness,' Falls rasped after the men were past, heading north on Front Street. 'How I wish I had more backbone!'

'You did just fine,' Steele said, moved to the door. 'If there were more people with your kind of guts maybe this town wouldn't have to put up with the kind of men who run the Blue Moon Saloon.'

There were two bolts on the front door of Falls' store. In full daylight, in firm control of his nervous tension, the pain in his arm starting to numb, Steele saw these and had no trouble in sliding them. Opened the door, undecided whether he would leave the premises by this exit or double back the way he had come.

Then he grunted, grimaced, started to bring the Colt Hartford to the aim as a shadow fell across the doorway. And a man appeared. Next a woman alongside him. He recognised the woman first: Doreen Jones in the unflattering men's clothing. And he checked the movement of the rifle when the man at her side said:

'There *are* enough men with guts and backbone to try to change things in this town, Steele! When ... Hell, now the time's right!'

Steele recognised him now: today attired in patched work clothes instead of professional mourning, as Charles Chambers had been when he was at the funeral of Arlene Forrester.

'Yessir, there most certainly are!'

Steele put a name to this voice before the side-whiskered Rufus Grimes came into view on the other side of Doreen from the mortician.

'Enough of us to see to it you get safe to Sheriff Fenton's office, Mr Steele,' another man said.

It took him a few moments to name this voice, until the man's wife augmented earnestly:

'Women, too, mister! Miss Doreen, she ain't the only female in Broadwater who's ready, willin' and able to come outta her kitchen. Stand up alongside the menfolk for what's right. When the time's right to do it.'

It was the couple who ran the restaurant where Steele ate yesterday. The Shiltons he recalled Doreen Jones had named them.

'Me and my good buddy ain't so young as we used to be. And one of us is lame. But we got our fair share of guts when needs be.'

Fulton Crabtree and Lars Johannsen had joined the expanding crowd of people out front of Falls' store.

149

Steele, his mind in unfamiliar turmoil as he struggled to come to terms with the totally unexpected, started to warn: 'I'm not sure all you people know what you're——'

He broke off as Falls, sweating as much as ever, his glasses removed, use the bottom of his apron to mop at the beads and runnels on his shiny face, slid out of the doorway past Steele, assured:

'Yes, sir. It's time we had somebody like you to show us the way. We'll——'

'He ain't a preacher, Howard!' Crabtree mocked.

Falls pulled a face, pressed on to make his point: 'We'll back you against those hooligans, Mr Steele. See you get your chance to talk turkey with Gavin Fenton.' He hooked his glasses back in place, lowered his voice to explain: 'I never knew about this when I let you into the storeroom.'

'And make sure the sheriff hears the truth about what happened at Gramps' place!' Doreen said emphatically. Added: 'Nobody knew this part of it was going to happen.'

The Virginian glanced over the eager array of a dozen faces, known and strange to him. Then looked out over the sparkling surface of the lake to the green hills beyond. At one dismissed from his racing mind the crazy theory he had somehow gotten hurt worse than by a small calibre slug tunnelling through a fleshy part of his arm. Struggled to readjust to the situation thrust upon him.

A man like yourself, Howard Falls had said without malice, surprised that somebody like Steele was able to reject the offered favours of an underage girl. Like he was the dregs of the earth, some kind of an outcast from decent society, a born troublemaker who was acting out of character.

In much the same way as the Garcia family were outcasts: simply because they were Mexicans. Which made them a type of people unwelcome in a quiet country community like Providence or even a wide open, anything goes town like Broadwater.

Decent people did not help the likes of the Garcias or himself. They had to take care of themselves: or of each other. Unless such outcasts happened to have reasons of their own for moving against what decent members of society abhorred and feared but felt powerless to confront themselves.

I appreciate your stand against the men who make this town the kind that encourages young girls to go wrong. Something else Howard Falls said in the darkened room out back of his store before he felt moved to take a hand in such a stand himself.

Steele had lent a helping hand to Esteban, Conchita and Maria Garcia. In doing so had gotten on the fighting side of the Blue Moon Saloon men whose methods of doing things were resented by the decent citizens of Broadwater. And a number of these citizens were ready to augment words with actions.

He looked back at the group which had expanded still further with men and women coming up from the southern stretch of Front Street and off the side streets that cut across town to rich California Avenue and the poverty row of Pacific beyond. Most he could not recall having seen before when he was in this town: a couple of storeclerks and some whose lines of business he could not readily identify by the clothes they wore. Also, Phil Turner and Jacko Buckman, the Red Dog partners of Benson and Small.

He did a double-take at these: checked their expressions— something close to smiles but too earnest to be exactly so—were not carefully manufactured for the occasion. Like the occasion itself certainly seemed to be manufactured. But, he was forced to acknowledge to himself, he ought to be able to benefit from this new turn of events. Because he could be in no worse trouble than he was already before the group congregated.

People began to talk all at once, competing with each other until their voices interlocked into a discord of sound from which nothing coherent emerged. Until Doreen Jones' voice became predominant, the others faltered and faded away.

'... will live with me forever. How you just pulled the knife out of the living flesh of that man! But men of your kind, who can stand up to the likes of those that make Mr Channon so powerful... I don't suppose you can afford to be so squeamish as others of us.'

'Be careful what you're sayin' to him, young lady,' a woman advised.

Doreen hurried on: 'And it didn't matter anyway, not when Mr Burnett and Mr Kildene and some of those others from the Blue Moon Saloon came into Gramps' cafe. Their rifles stinking of gunsmoke. Bossing around Deputy Rawlings like he was nothing and they were the law or something!'

'You tell him, Miss Doreen!' Fulton Crabtree urged when the woman paused for breath.

'Maybe if you are silent, Miss Doreen will be able to tell him, my good old friend,' Lars Johannsen suggested, faintly mocking.

'Hot damn, let's get on with it!' the lame man countered, thudding both sticks against the sidewalk.

'Well, Mr Steele,' Doreen continued, nodding in agreement with both old-timers. 'I'd seen you come into the back of Mr Falls' store and after I'd listened to those men and watched them for just a minute, I knew it was now or never that the people of this town made a stand. It wouldn't have mattered that Deputy Rawlings was around. If they'd found you, they'd have lynched you, Mr Steele. And you didn't do anything you didn't have to in Gramps' place, and——'

'Except, perhaps, to knock down an old man like me!' a familiarly thick Welsh accented voice complained from the back of the crowd.

Doreen was both surprised and anxious that her grandfather had joined the group. As Crabtree, attempting with little success to mimic the other man's accent, chided: 'You can shut up for a change, Jones the cafe!'

'Not before I have told this boyo here I overlook what he did. He did it for a good reason, so I——'

'Yeah, Gramps, okay!' Doreen cut in. Abruptly reached out a hand toward the undertaker, who took it without embarrassment as they exchanged affectionate looks.

Even in his present confused state of mind over what was happening so fast, Steele had time to feel resentment toward

Chambers. Which was absolutely crazy, he knew, as the woman went on:

'It was mine and Charles' idea, Mr Steele. Charles—Mr Chambers—had heard a lot about you from going to Providence so often to bury people who——'

'Not always on account of you, of course,' Chambers hurried to correct any possible misinterpretation.

'Anyway, what does all that matter?' Doreen said. 'The reason I brought you to the cafe after the trouble this morning, we were going to ask you to help. After what happened at Gramps', well, things started to happen so fast.'

'And now it is you need help as much as us, I think?' Lars Johannsen suggested, his quizzical expression adding the query.

'It's up to you, Mr Steele,' Doreen said, disengaged her hand from Chambers', looked imperiously around to establish that she truly spoke for her fellow citizens. 'We think we should see you get into the custody of Sheriff Fenton. He's as honest a lawman as a town with Channon so powerful is likely to have. We can fight your case, stand up to——'

'We've talked enough, I figure!' Rufus Grimes broke in, half drew a revolver from a side pocket of his pants.

Other men showed themselves also to be armed with handguns: pushed into the waistbands of their pants, stuck through their belts or jutting out of pockets like that of Grimes.

Steele once more peered out across the lake. This time felt as if he were caught up in some kind of brightly sunlit nightmare in which he had no control over events that rolled him hell for leather toward his destiny. A situation, too, it seemed, that was also getting out of control of the people crowded before the haberdashery store: who were eager only to set things moving even faster, uncaring about the eventual outcome. Which, in their present states of mind, they doubtless considered could be no worse than it was right now.

'What do you say, Mr Steele?' Howard Falls asked, his tone of voice strong, his courage boosted at seeing that so

153

many of his fellow citizens thought along the same lines as he did.

But what was that line? Did they truly intend to escort him into the questionable safety of a cell behind the law office up at the other end of Front Street? Or, if they did, were they open to a change of plan? Because he certainly had no intention of allowing the law to take its course: assuming the law were given the opportunity.

Like hell! For, he knew, with this motley bunch of unlikely partners to back his play he had a far better chance to resolve his own problems with the men who ran Broadwater—the lawmen and the moneymen—than if he were alone.

'What the hell's happening down there?' another familiar voice demanded. From a greater distance.

The Virginian looked north along a deserted stretch of Front Street to where Gavin Fenton stood, flanked by Dexter and Rawlings, at a point where the shore line bulged out into the lake. And as he watched, along with the group of local citizens gathered on the sidewalk behind him, this trio of lawmen was joined by two more who moved out into the centre of Broadwater's main thoroughfare from an adjacent side street. The metal badges on the shirt fronts of all five men glinted in the early afternoon sunlight.

'Well, boyo, do we help each other or not?' David Jones asked.

'I reckon we're past the point of no return on that,' Steele said. Moved off the store threshold, crossed the sidewalk, stepped down on to the street. 'Only the one way we can go.'

'Let us hope it is the right way,' Lars Johannsen said tautly.

'Any man who doesn't believe it is shouldn't be here,' Charles Chambers countered grimly.

Steele sloped the Colt Hartford to the shoulder above his good arm, rested his thumb over the hammer.

'For God's sake, let's get movin'!' Howard Falls urged, his voice shrill with tension, sweat beading his face again.

Fulton Crabtree growled: 'For God's sake let's hope there's not the devil to pay, uh, Mr Steele?'

The Virginian drawled: 'With those two fellers waiting for us to arrive, I reckon it surely is better to travel hopefully.'

154

13

As he started toward the line of lawmen strung out across the broad width of Front Street, Adam Steele reflected briefly upon his mixed feelings for the town of Broadwater. An ambivalence triggered on the one hand by the conviction he had taken the right course in choosing to settle for the life of a horsebreeder on a country stud ranch, on the other by an occasional difficulty to resist hankering to indulge himself as a high-rolling gambling man under the bright lights of the plush kind of place he knew the Blue Moon Saloon to be.

This insistent line of thought was then allied to some others that gripped him just as firmly for stretched seconds as he progressed further along the centre of the street between the curving line of commercial enterprises and the expanse of calm, crystal clear water for which the town was named.

It was not the first time he had taken such a tense walk along the dusty street of a western town—and right now he did not take into account today's earlier trouble when he rode his gelding toward the quartet of Blue Moon Saloon men.

It was the kind of confrontation he had been a part of in many communities: but although it was familiar, yet it was also odd.

For never before had he been backed by such an ill-assorted bunch of mostly old men. All surely totally inexperienced in such a situation, fraught with the risk of sudden death: so having to handle a series of sensations that were unlike any they had felt before. Their minds and bodies reacting every passing moment to countless previously unknown responses triggered by a new brand of fear.

Never before, either, had Steele gone up against the likes of

155

Gavin Fenton and the sheriff's four deputies. Lawmen who, he understood, were respected by the decent people of the town.

Now he no longer felt like he was caught up in a nightmare. Nor experiencing an hallucination caused by a mystery injury he did not know he suffered. There was a dreamlike quality about the afternoon. He felt he was split in two. One part of him a tangible flesh and blood feature of the tableau: out front of the group of a score or more resolute greenhorns, heading for a showdown with five men who were surely as expert as he was in such a situation. While another part of him had become detached from his physical being: witnessed the scene from the sidelines. Both parts seeing it all a little fuzzily, hearing the accompanying sounds slightly distorted.

Gavin Fenton spoke as the gap between him and his flanking deputies and Steele and the men who crowded closer to the Virginian closed to sixty feet or so.

'That's fine. I don't have to shout at you people any more.'

Abruptly, as the two separated parts of Steele became one again, the sense of being in a dream vanished and he recalled hearing this same voice—familiar but not identifiable— booming along the street, demanding to know what was happening out front of Howard Falls' store.

And Steele suddenly felt good about the way things had turned out: for the first time since he pushed open the swing door and stepped into the cafe kitchen. Confident that whatever the outcome, he had adapted as best he could to the rapidly changing situation. Called his own moves just right so that he was now this close to getting what he had returned to this town to achieve.

He let a few stretched seconds pass, swept his gaze back and forth along the line of lawmen who stood, apparently at their ease but doubtless achingly tense in back of the façades. The metal of the guns jutting from their holsters sparkling in the sunlight as brightly as their badges of office. Their faces were hard but, he chose to believe, honest. They were men who would draw and kill in two clearly defined circumstances: in self defence or when they were certain what they were doing was justified.

Which gave Steele an affinity with them.

This established, he glanced over each shoulder in turn at the men behind him. Could not be sure, but thought he may have collected a few more greenhorn gunfighters on the way up the street from the haberdashery store. All returned his impassive gaze with expressions that ranged from eager to fearful. None spoke, the nearest any of them got to saying anything was to nod, in ways that assured him they were prepared to go along with anything he said or did.

Which, the stray thought occurred to him, showed more faith than he would have placed in a stranger in any situation that could in a moment turn into one of life or death.

'It seems you're elected spokesman, Steele,' Fenton said. Made a pouting shape with his lips, a low sucking noise that maybe indicated he wished he was back sitting behind his desk, drawing against the pipe, in a situation over which he held firm control. 'So why don't you go ahead and tell me why I shouldn't arrest you for the murder of Buddy Benson?'

'How about because I had to kill him in self defence, Sheriff?'

Fenton pursed his lips again, but this time not in wishful thinking about a pipeful of cool smoking tobacco. Rather as an unconscious sign he was making a decision about which he was unsure. Then he said: 'I just have your word for that?'

'You can have mine as well, boyo!' David Jones put in quickly. 'And the word of my granddaughter, too. Both of us were eye witnesses to what happened. As we told your deputy when he and those——'

'And mine and Lars!' Fulton Crabtree growled thickly. 'Not eye witnesses, exactly. But we heard most of what went on, Mr Fenton.'

Fenton listened a little impatiently to these assurances, then asked: 'In that case, with all those witnesses to back your word, why did you make yourself a fugitive and run away, Steele?'

The numbness was starting to go from the bullet wound in Steele's arm. As it hurt worse, he was vaguely troubled by the notion of infection. Maybe even gangrene. But it was too early for this to have taken a hold yet.

157

'When it all happened, he had no reason to expect anybody would speak up for him!' David Jones argued.

'Gramps, I'm asking the man to speak up for himself now,' Fenton said, his tone low but hard, his time-lined face expressing curiosity.

'I went looking for the men who killed Billy Small in mistake for me,' the Virginian said, allowed his gaze to become fixed on the red-headed deputy named Rawlings whom he had mistaken for the sheriff when he heard him at the cafe.

The man was disconcerted for a moment, then was again as impassive as Dexter, the other two older deputies and Fenton himself: after he had shot a quizzical glance toward the sheriff, seen a tacit signal that he should remain silent.

'I'm treating that as a separate crime for the moment. Even though Paul Rawlings tells me it looks like Small was shot down by a rifle.'

He fixed his gaze for a moment on the Colt Hartford canted to Steele's shoulder.

'*A* friggin' rifle?' a man behind Steele snarled.

'Everybody heard a whole——' Chambers started.

Howard Falls interrupted him: 'Mr Fenton, I can tell you who——'

'Sheriff?' Steele said.

'Steele?'

'If you're set on arresting me, then that's what you're going to try to do, I reckon. But I have to tell you. The kind of town this is, the kind of men who run around loose in it, I'm not going to come quietly. Let myself be locked up in one of your cells that have windows on to a side alley.'

'Is that a threat, Steele?' Fenton's eyes glowered, his mouth adopted a hard line.

'No, it's just a statement of fact, Sheriff.'

Fenton sucked in his cheeks, ballooned them, allowed the air to rasp out of pursed lips. This time it was like he was smoking again. Before he said: 'What if I don't arrest you? Don't give you call to use that fancy rifle against me and my deputies the way you used it against the Blue Moon Saloon boys up on Fourteenth Street this morning?'

Steele nodded, said evenly: 'Then I'll just go about the business I have at the Blue Moon Saloon.'

'Can I ask the nature of that business?'

Steele's mind was filled with an image of the imploring faces of Esteban, Conchita and Maria Garcia. He dismissed it in a moment, just a fleeting frown signalling his irritability. For another moment wondered if Doreen Jones' claim to know about Carmelita Garcia's connection with Robert Casper Channon had been anything more than bait. He said to Fenton:

'I have to be sure if I ever need to come to this town again neither Channon nor any of his hired muscle will try to prevent it.'

Now a frown came to Fenton's face, took firm hold on his sun burnished features when he growled: 'We've already talked about that, Steele! Luke Dexter's order for you to leave town has been rescinded. It's now just a matter of whether you're guilty or innocent of murder. Whether you stay here in Broadwater, locked up in the jailhouse: where I'll guarantee your safety. Or you convince me you're not guilty. In which case you'll be free to come and go as you please in this town.'

'I told you, boyo, the man's innocent of——'

Fenton made a sudden decision, held up a hand to interrupt Jones. Said: 'All right, I know you're no passing through saddletramp, Steele. And you're not about to take a powder away from what you've built up on the old Sanderson place down near Providence. Since there are two eye witnesses to speak for you. And two more who heard what went on at Gramps' place. I'll go along with you being innocent. Unless I find out something different after I've looked into the killings myself. So you can turn around now, go on back home, Steele. Allows time for things between you and the Blue Moon Saloon boys to cool off.'

'I can't do that, Sheriff,' Steele told him.

It was clear the lawman had expected a negative response. The hand he had raised in a silencing gesture, kept aloft while he spoke, came back down to his shirt pocket. He slowly took out the ready filled pipe and a match, his features pensive as

159

he gave further thought to his decision, finally admitted:

'No, I didn't think you'd do that, Steele. But keep this in mind. Don't step out of line in doing your business at the Blue Moon Saloon. Me and these men will be watching to see you don't. While we do our duty, you understand? Find the men who killed Billy Small.'

'Sure,' Steele answered. 'It's your town, so you can do most of what you like.'

Fenton struck the match on the butt of his sixgun, held it in one hand, pipe in the other, shook his head as he countered: 'No, it's not my town, Steele.' He peered back over his shoulder, along the curve of Front Street. Beyond where Steele and the men behind him were able to see, but they all knew the Blue Moon Saloon was the predominant building up there. 'No town ought to be anybody's town.'

The Virginian answered evenly: 'Like nobody ought to belong to anybody else.'

14

The sheriff and four deputies all glowered at Steele, the two older men even made moves toward drawing their holstered revolvers.

'He doesn't mean that like it sounds!' Charles Chambers blurted and the fear that was a lump in his throat could be heard in the way his voice squeaked.

'Hold it, you guys!' Fenton snapped. Shot a glance to left and right. Waited until most of the tension had drained away, then touched the match flame to the tobacco in the pipe bowl, drew against it with long intakes of breath. Dropped the match, said on a stream of expelled smoke: 'He for sure meant it like it sounded. So I guess me and my deputies'll have to show him he's more wrong than a three dollar bill.'

He peered meaningfully at the group of men behind Steele, then over his shoulder along the inland curving stretch of Front Street, suddenly swung into a half turn, moved on to the side street. The others responded to something he rasped at them, fell in behind him. Spared no glances north along the street, directed grim stares toward Steele.

Fulton Crabtree announced with a tone of awe: 'Mr Steele, we heard tell from folks who know of the kinda trouble you been in down around Povidence how you believe in livin' dangerous. But rubbin' Gavin Fenton up the wrong way just when you got him on your side, that was damn fool crazy, seems to me.'

'Sometimes the truth is daft, boyo,' David Jones said.

'And sometimes it hurts,' Howard Falls added.

Steele moved forward, was aware of few following footfalls

161

at first. Within a few moments, though, all the men had chosen to trail behind him again. Near as he could judge without looking back at them. Which he did not do after he glanced down the side street where Fenton and the deputies had gone, saw it was empty: of lawmen or anyone else. Then surveyed Front Street up to the three-story façade of the Blue Moon Saloon and beyond. It was just as deserted: but a lot more dangerous.

Charles Chambers said grimly: 'If it's only feelings get hurt this afternoon, it'll be a lucky day for all concerned, I'd say.'

'That sure is right, isn't it, Mr Steele?' Rufus Grimes added.

The Virginian looked down at his left shirt sleeve crusted with congealed blood, smiled grimly to himself, drawled: 'Just hope we're all as thick skinned as I am. Already been deeply wounded and survived.'

Because he had lived in the small town of Providence for so long, and on account of his recent experiences of Broadwater, Steele knew of the speed with which news could travel through such communities. And maybe some kind of record was set this afternoon. For the utter silence that was clamped over this usually busy town squeezed between the lake shore on the west and the steep slope to the east seemed to suggest that every soul here was tensely conscious of a momentous event about to take place.

The vast majority of people, it seemed, had elected simply to keep off the streets, await the outcome at a distance. But many, Steele was sure, were concealed in vantage points from which they could watch the climax of his trouble with the men of the Blue Moon Saloon. And, he could not help feeling, a large proportion of these watchers would be less than satisfied with the result unless it entailed a blood-letting.

Such thoughts came and went through his mind as he narrowed the distance on the Blue Moon Saloon. Feeling good that on the main street of Broadwater he needed only to remain alert to potential danger from one side. The open beach and the mirror-smooth lake to his left side offered nowhere from which to spring an ambush.

So he kept careful watch just to one side and ahead. Did

not concern himself with what was behind. Because he did not think even the kind of men who gunned down a man coming out of a doorway at first glimpse would have the gall to bushwhack the group from behind in such a public place as this. Too, these men with him, Steele guessed, instinctively spent much time looking over their shoulders. Although how many searched for hidden guns, how many cast anxious glances at the bunch of women moving along the side of the street three hundred feet away he did not know.

Just as he could not decide what proportion of the hidden eager watchers were troubled by whose blood was let in the shoot-out they were certain was imminent. Hidden in saloons, hotels, casinos, whorehouses, dancehalls and all kinds of stores. Establishments which perhaps gained in one way or another much from the existence of the Blue Moon Saloon as Broadwater's prime attraction. Could lose out if something happened at the place that caused this to become a different kind of town.

This was not Steele's aim, of course. Although, he had to allow, it probably was in the minds of David Jones, Howard Falls and a few of the other devoutly religious men who were backing him.

It was too late now to state his motives, though: and even if he had the time, he probably would not have used it to explain the plain and simple truth of what he was about.

He reached a point, on the centre of the street, directly opposite the double glass-panelled doors of the Blue Moon. The entrance through which Esteban Garcia had been ejected by Whitey Burnett yesterday. Here he halted, turned to face the large building, its many windows glinting in the afternoon sunlight. Then, after a brief exchange of low-toned talk opened by Fulton Crabtree, encouraged by Lars Johannsen, the men spread out to either side of him. Formed a line in the manner of the Blue Moon Saloon men this morning, the lawmen this afternoon. But longer, and aligned down the centre of the street rather than across it.

When the shuffling into position was completed there was silence. And for many moments all that moved were the billows of disturbed dust settling on and around the booted feet that had kicked it up.

Steele looked to his left, saw Chambers immediately beside him, Crabtree, Grimes and Johannsen beyond, then others. Closest to him on his right stood David Jones, Howard Falls, then Turner and Buckman and the rest.

They were the most unlikely looking bunch of gunmen Steele had ever seen.

A block along the street, beyond the corner of the Blue Moon Saloon, was a larger group of women than had gathered down at the store at the start, and a few men.

A glance in the other direction failed to show him Fenton or any of the deputies. Nor anybody else. He turned to face the hotel, called:

'I have some business with Robert C. Channon!'

His voice bounced off the façade of the building like an echo. Or maybe it only seemed to be that way in the minds of the men lined up on the centre of the street: their tension such they heard and saw more clearly in imagination than reality.

Steele raked his gaze from one end of the building façade to the other. After perhaps ten seconds gave an emphatic nod, yelled in a more strident tone: 'All right, Mr Channon! Maybe you aren't too keen on public speaking! I'll come on in! We can talk in private!'

He looked to left and right, growled: 'Stay here.'

Did not wait for any kind of acknowledgement before he stepped out of the line, headed for the glass-panelled doors. Came to a halt after three paces when the doors were flung open with great force and another member of the Garcia family came powering out from between them.

There was no label on her but he would have bet the Trail's End spread to a dime the slim-bodied, beautiful, tearfully-terrified woman who lunged toward him was Carmelita Garcia.

She was forced by the impetus of a vicious shove in the back to stagger across the sidewalk. Made the step down on to the street, but could no longer remain on her feet after this. So pitched to the ground and rolled amid a cloud of dust. In such a way the skirt of her dress was dragged up around her slender thighs. She writhed, sobbed in pain and humiliation, then jerked at the dress to cover herself. Sobbed more forcefully, vented a string of fast spoken Mexican-Spanish Steele thought he would recognise as obscenities if he had paid more attention to some of what Esteban Garcia had blurted in times of high tension.

He raised his gaze from the woman as she curled herself into a ball, covered her head with her hands, became almost silent. Peered at the hotel entrance where the doors would have swung closed after banging against the outside walls to either side. Were prevented from doing this by the outstretched hands of Whitey Burnett on the left, Kildene on the right. Then they lowered their hands, held them near holstered revolvers as their narrow-eyed gazes raked along the line of men behind Steele and the woman, challenging them to draw. But the handguns remained thrust inside pockets, waistbands and under belts.

'Funny, ain't it?' Burnett mocked with a brutal grin.

'I don't hear anyone laughing,' Steele said.

'The way you always seem to happen by the Blue Moon just when we're throwin' out the garbage?'

Steele took two more steps forward, and Burnett and Kildene became rigid with tension, poised to draw, an instant away from dropping into gunfighter's crouches. But they relaxed when Steele went down on his haunches, used his free hand—the top of the arm above it protesting the movement—to grip the shoulder of the Mexican woman. She looked up at him then, her terror at his touch suddenly as great as when she was sent staggering out of the hotel.

'You're Carmelita Garcia?'

She tried to speak, failed to find her voice, nodded and fisted wetness out of her eyes.

He showed her a momentary smile, told her: 'You're going to get up on your feet. Go down the street to where those women are waiting.'

He gestured along Front Street.

She looked in the same south direction, swallowed hard,

165

rasped: '*Si, señor*. I will try. *Gracias*.'

He thought that without his help, which cost him a lot of pain from his gunshot arm, she would not have made it to her feet. But when she did she seemed to draw strength from the achievement. Then even more when she looked around, saw the line of men behind Steele, the grinning Burnett and the glowering Kildene in the doorway. She took a few tentative steps, broke into an ungainly run that quickly became fluid. Some of the women came forward to meet and help her. Steele did not see who, returned his full attention to Burnett when the white-haired man said:

'You got what you came for, uh? Way it is, that Mex dame wasn't workin' out so hot in the rooms after Mr Channon tired of her anyways. So you're welcome to have her. You can beat it now, take her home to her old man, okay?'

'No.'

'What d'you mean, no?' Burnett was genuinely perturbed by Steele's negative response.

'The lady wasn't my business with Channon.'

'*Mister* Channon don't have no other kinda business with you!' Burnett snarled. 'He's a mite peeved at how you killed a couple of his boys this mornin'! Maybe, too, you would've killed me and Kenny Kildene here if the sheriff hadn't happened by?'

'Channon in the hotel right now?'

'What the frig is that to you?'

'If I have to go some place else to do my business with him, I'd like to know where.'

'Where you can go, Steele, is to hell!' Kildene snarled. 'Right, Whitey?'

'And we're the guys that'll send him there if he tries to come into the Blue Moon, Kenny,' Burnett growled with mounting confidence.

An attitude, Steele was sure, which revealed the white-haired man had received some kind of signal. Then everyone else was shown a far less subtle sign. For several windows were suddenly, forcefully, slammed open. And a rifle barrel was thrust out through each of these, the men behind the guns no more than dark shadows behind the lace curtains. All the rifles swung back and forth, constantly moving from Steele to the abruptly much more frightened men in the line along the centre of the street behind him.

'Oh, my God!' Howard Falls muttered.

'Hot damn!' Fulton Crabtree rasped.

Lars Johannsen said something in his native language in much the same tone as when David Jones cursed in Welsh or the Garcia husband and wife in Mexican-Spanish.

Other men gasped, groaned or grunted. Someone said into the stillness that lasted for a stretched second in the wake of the other expressions of shock:

'Aw shit!'

Steele had figured the men of the Blue Moon Saloon would be ready to make a stand, if that was what Robert Channon wanted them to make. The gathering of the greenhorns, then the exchanges with Fenton and his deputies had allowed ample time for this. But Steele had not expected them to show their hand in such a way. Out here on the open street. In the full glare of sunlight beating down out of the western half of the sky. Within sight of a large proportion of Broadwater's citizens.

Especially not after Channon had sanctioned the handing over of Carmelita Garcia without a fight. That had seemed to be a sure sign the man wanted no more trouble.

And Steele had called it wrong. He should have backed off with what he had. Lived to fight another day on the issue of his freedom to come and go in Broadwater.

In calling it wrong, he had been influenced by what could turn out to be a fatal misinterpretation of Gavin Fenton's part in the showdown. For it seemed the lawman did not intend to turn just a blind eye. He had turned his back to it.

'See, Mister Horse's Ass Rancher,' Burnett crowed, 'this here Blue Moon Saloon is private property. Open to the public, sure. But the management is entitled to reserve right of admission. And the management ain't never again admittin' no Mexicans—male nor female, neither. Nor no troublemakers who tote around fancy rifles just lookin' for chances to use 'em.'

'Has Channon——'

167

'Listen, frig it, I ain't through speakin' my piece yet!' Burnett bellowed across Steele's even-toned interruption. 'Any greasers try to come in here, we'll toss 'em out like always. A rifle-totin' troublemaker tries it, well ... We'll use a little extra force on him. And if Gavin Fenton reckons we use too much of that kinda persuadin' we can always say it was self-defence. The way you claimed it was that when you knifed Buddy Benson and blasted all that lead into Billy Small.'

As if in response to another signal, the five rifles angled down toward the same target: Adam Steele. This as the Virginian recognised the men who had helped him get this far toward securing his ends had become a liability. For in planning his next move he had to take into account all those lives on the line: that any aggression by him was sure to bring violent retaliation.

But then this consideration was driven out of his mind as he faced the inevitable fact he would be the first to die in such a gun battle if the others attempted to back him. And if they went down as they tried, they would have made their own decisions. So the hell with it. Freedom to choose without bowing to the dictates of big money power and fear of the guns that power bought was what this whole thing was about.

He stepped forward, on to the patch of ground where Carmelita Garcia had stirred up the dust.

Burnett's confidence drained out of him and his taunting grin became a scowl as he snarled: 'I'm warnin' you, mister!'

'And we warn you, sir!' Rufus Grimes counter challenged. And within the time it took him to speak these few mono-syllables his voice came down half an octave in pitch.

Which took him by surprise, and while the side-whiskered man came to terms with being able to sound as forceful out here on the dangerous street as when he conducted an auction, David Jones filled the pause, growled:

'Right, boyo!'

'We don't want no more killin' in this town, that's what we warn you Blue Moon people!' Fulton Crabtree snarled.

'That is correct,' Lars Johannsen added.

Burnett and Kildene grew tenser with each challenge issued by the line of less than impressive looking greenhorn gunmen. Clerks and merchants, businessmen and small-time gamblers: dressed in dungarees and aprons, coveralls and shabby suits, battered Stetsons and dented Derbies. All showing the butts of guns that were far from new, probably had not been fired in a long time, if ever, and never in anger.

A low murmuring of more talk rippled along the line of men as they saw the unease of the two in the hotel doorway. But none of them made a move to draw his gun, or advance on the Blue Moon Saloon.

From the upper two stories of the hotel, at the windows where the riflemen stood, there came no sound. A couple of rifles wavered in their downward aim at Steele, like the hands that held them shook.

Kenny Kildene had started to get angry. Now shifted his gaze away from running back and forth along the line of men. Stared demandingly at Burnett, who was still as anxious as he became at the moment Steele elected not to back off from the aimed rifles. Which was obviously when he had expected the confrontation to end. His instructions had apparently not taken account of events beyond this point. There were no more pre-arranged signals to chart his course of action.

As Steele realised this he experienced a feeling that approached euphoria. Which caused him to act on the kind of impulse that in another set of circumstances he would have rejected as stupidly reckless.

He started another step forward. Drew an immediate response from the nervous Kildene. Who reached for his gun. Had the revolver clawed out of the holster, but just half cocked and not yet levelled, when the Colt Hartford barrel thudded into the open palm of Steele's left hand.

The Virginian winced as the force of the impact travelled the length of his arm to the bullet hole at the top. But his expression was mild compared with the look of mixed surprise, fear and an instant of pain that was fixed on the face of Kenny Kildene when the shot from the Colt Hartford tunnelled a bullet deep into his chest.

At a range of less than thirty feet the rifle shot had enough velocity to drive the man into a backward stagger, still holding his gun, but without the strength to drag it up, its weight suddenly increased out of all proportion. He went down hard, sprawled on his back, became utterly still except for the blood oozing out of the hole in his chest.

Burnett was gripped by mindless rage. Compounded of every evil thought he had nurtured toward Adam Steele, from that first moment twenty four hours ago when he was knocked down by the Virginian's rifle barrel. On this very spot.

Buddy Benson had been spurred by a similar massive force of ill will toward Steele when he fired his small-calibre gambler's gun across the kitchen of the Red Lion Cafe. But his gun had been drawn.

Burnett, who was surely a fast draw, needed to reach for his Colt. And because of his raging emotions, haste hampered speed. He did everything right: except to be angry. When his gun came to the aim he had time to start to squeeze the trigger. But a fraction of a second earlier, the Colt Hartford had fired another shot. The bullet blasted into the belly of Burnett and as he folded forward the revolver in his hand sent its shot into the front of the sidewalk, exploded a spray of splinters. He remained standing unsteadily on widely splayed legs.

In the fleeting moments of time it required for Steele to finish the two men at the hotel entrance he was totally detached from the danger of the rifles aimed on him from above. But as more seconds slipped away into the silence he knew just his own rifle and Burnett's revolver had been fired to shatter the stillness of the afternoon.

Gunsmoke drifted, its acrid taint quickly lost in the clear mountain air on the shore of the lake.

Whitey Burnett tried to fold himself upright, but he managed only to raise his head, showed a look of nothing more than mild dislike to Steele, said: 'Ain't there nothin' you do that ain't friggin' right?'

He tried to bring his gun to the aim with both hands.

170

Realised it would take more strength than he had. So let the Colt fall to the floor in the doorway where the trouble with Steele had started and, he had to know, was about to end. Clutched with both hands at the blossoming stain at his belly as the Virginian replied:

'Plenty, feller. But I do my best to avoid making any fatal mistakes.'

Because of the threatening rifles above, he did not as usual cant the Colt Hartford back to his shoulder. That might have been misinterpreted by the men on the upper floors, so he angled it downwards as Burnett crumpled to the carpeted floor just inside the plush lobby of the Blue Moon Saloon. Tilted his head up and saw, in fact, he was no longer covered by the rifles at the windows. They were now aimed again at the line of men on the centre of the street, tracked back and forth without haste.

Then he turned his head slowly, saw all his erstwhile helpers with their hands raised high in the air, stretched to the limit to emphasise they had no intention of taking a violent hand in the trouble. Even Fulton Crabtree, who needed two sticks to walk, could stand still without them. On their faces were expressions that varied from shame to fear, but these gradually changed to confusion and curiosity. Then all showed a mixture of relief and pleasant surprise as mass attention was focused on one window.

Steele looked up there, too. Where the rifle barrel had been withdrawn and the time-lined face under greying curly hair of Gavin Fenton appeared from behind the net curtains.

The lawman peered down at Steele with an earnest expression, had no need to raise his voice in the brittle silence that seemed to have a palpable presence out front of the hotel.

'I'm glad you didn't get hurt in this, Steele.'

The Virginian answered in a matching even tone: 'I'm glad to see I finished up on the side of law and order.'

Fenton almost spoke with impulsive anger, but stopped himself. Gave an almost imperceptible nod as he said: 'Law is for the protection of the people. All of them. Why I and my deputies had to take a hand in this. Prevent those men out on

171

the street from doing anything that could have got them hurt.'

'I'm grateful, Sheriff.'

'Me, too, Steele,' the lawman replied, and although his face was void of expression, he managed to convey with those three short words a much longer message.

Or so Steele chose to infer as Fenton withdrew from the window and he turned away from the hotel entrance: aware of the other four rifles going from sight as Dexter and Rawlings and the two older deputies responded to the sheriff's lead. And the men on the centre of the street lowered their arms, vented a series of sighs and grunts and groans.

'Ain't no one as thankful as you, Charlie Chambers!' somebody challenged from within the hotel. On the ground floor, not far back from the lobby through the open double doors where the two inert corpses lay. 'I count that's six money-makin' corpses that hot-shot rifleman from Providence has give you! Why, I bet if——'

'Silence!' another man boomed. And as the command was instantly obeyed Steele guessed the speaker was Robert Caspar Channon. Realised this was the first time he had heard the man's voice: and he had yet to see him in the flesh.

Then a moon-faced, wall-eyed fat woman of middle years dressed in a bib apron straining at the seams appeared in the lobby. Carefully moved around the corpses to the doors, pulled them closed.

'That hired muscleman isn't right, you know,' somebody said.

Steele turned away from the hotel once more, saw that most of the men were drifting off along Front Street: some looking as weary as if they had done a day's gruelling work, which maybe such greenhorns had, while others seemed strangely invigorated by what they had been a part of.

It was the pale-faced, bug-eyed, pot-bellied Chambers who came toward Steele, showed righteous indignation as he expanded on his rebuttal of the taunt: 'I'm never thankful to bury anybody. It's a job somebody has to do and I do it.'

Steele nodded, replied: 'Like me and killing people sometimes, feller.'

They both looked at Doreen Jones as she fell in between them after moving against the tide of people on the street.

The undertaker went on: 'You did what was necessary, Mr Steele.' He jerked a thumb back toward the Blue Moon Saloon. 'I don't know if you'll ever be welcome in that place, bu. I don't think anyone will try to stop you doing whatever else you want to do in Broadwater. Providing it's legal, of course.'

'It's what it was all about,' Steele said.

Doreen Jones said a little breathlessly: 'That's good.'

'And I'm sure Gavin Fenton thinks so, too,' Chambers muttered. 'I'm pretty sure he was willing to back whichever side won, but he was hoping for things to turn out this way.'

'Reckon you're right, feller.'

'Mr Steele?' The slender bodied, almost good-looking Doreen eyed the Virginian nervously.

'Where's my horse, ma'am?'

She blinked, momentarily perplexed by mention of a subject not in her mind. Then: 'Oh, still tied to Gramps' wagon out front of the cafe, far as I know. There's something else.'

He nodded: 'I don't see *Señora* Garcia anyplace?'

'Yes, that's it, Mr Steele. Carmelita Garcia went willingly to be Channon's mistress. And she chose to stay and work at the Blue Moon when that awful creep found himself a new love. She's run off from us. I don't know where she'll go. But I'm sure she won't ever settle for being the wife of a peon after the kind of life she had here in this town.'

Steele reflected upon how Doreen Jones had not exactly lied, not exactly told him the truth to have him ride with her to the Red Lion Cafe. But in the light of everything else, that didn't seem important. He said to her:

'What her husband and daughters do about that is up to them.'

'You want me to patch up that arm, Mr Steele?' the woman asked as Chambers took her hand in his.

The Virginian fleetingly recalled his thoughts, after the funeral of Arlene Forrester, about getting another woman to

173

take her place: even a wife. Shook his head at the idea and in response to the query, added: 'Thanks, but that's one little thing I reckon I can take care of myself.'

'Okay. I guess, anyway, I'm more suited to help Charles and Gramps take care of the bullet holes in the kitchen. Before we finish painting up the place.'

She lengthened her stride, forcing Chambers to match her increased pace. Looked back to call to the Virginian: 'Next time you come to Broadwater, you be sure to stop by Gramps' place. Sample some of that fine food you never got around to eating this visit.'

Steele used the hand holding the rifle to tip his hat.

A little further down the street, Fulton Crabtree peered out over the batwing doors of one of Broadwater's smaller saloons. Raised a glass of beer in the manner of a toast as he called:

'Hey, Mr Steele. I want to thank you for allowin' me to have a hand in that: an old buzzard with a game leg like me. It was real excitin' while it lasted.'

'Whatever you say, feller,' the Virginian replied flatly as he went on by the saloon entrance. 'My opinion, it's a matter of bad things being like the good. They all have to...

... COME TO AN END.'*

*As does this Adam Steele episode. Watch out for the next one to begin.

174

GEORGE G. GILMAN

EDGE 55: UNEASY RIDERS

She was one of those Liberating women.

Right now it was horses she was trying to liberate. Two of them, rightfully the property of the lawmen who'd just awakened the man called Edge and told him that *his* horse had been liberated by a night-time thief who'd been liberated from Nebraska's Carlsburg Penitentiary by his brothers-in-outlawry.

Altogether too much liberation going on.

Edge looked at the woman. She'd ambushed them like a man, handled a rifle like a man. Was dressed in a man's clothes – tho' she filled them just like a woman.

There and then he decided that this Woman's Movement had to be stopped in its tracks. Stopped dead if necessary.

POST A LITTLE HAPPINESS

Post·A·Book

A Royal Mail service in association with the Book Marketing Council & The Booksellers Association.
Post-A-Book is a Post Office trademark.

MORE WESTERNS AVAILABLE FROM
HODDER AND STOUGHTON PAPERBACKS

GEORGE G. GILMAN

☐	05825 5	Edge 49: Revenge Ride	£1.50
☐	05901 4	Edge 51: A Time for Killing	£1.50
☐	40417 X	Edge 54: Backshot	£1.75
☐	41105 2	Edge 55: Uneasy Riders	£1.75

STEELE SERIES

☐	39035 7	Steele 41: The Killing Strain	£1.50
☐	40228 2	Steele 42: The Big Gunfight	£1.95
☐	40846 9	Steele 43: The Hunted	£1.95
☐	41203 2	Steele 44: Code of the West	£1.95

All these books are available at your local bookshop or newsagent, or can be ordered direct from the publisher. Just tick the titles you want and fill in the form below.

Prices and availability subject to change without notice.

Hodder & Stoughton Paperbacks, P.O. Box 11, Falmouth, Cornwall

Please send cheque or postal order, and allow the following for postage and packing:

U.K. – 55p for one book, plus 22p for the second book, and 14p for each additional book ordered up to a £1.75 maximum.

B.F.P.O. and EIRE – 55p for the first book, plus 22p for the second book, and 14p per copy for the next 7 books, 8p per book thereafter.

OTHER OVERSEAS CUSTOMERS – £1.00 for the first book, plus 25p per copy for each additional book.

Name ....

Address ....

....